Manson Wanted to Live Here

Flipped

My name is Jamie and I'm a coward. I wasn't always a coward. I remember the day I started becoming a coward. It was the day I had a four-wheeler on top of me.

Let me clarify my definition of the word "coward" for the purpose of my story: a coward is someone who is afraid or reluctant to leave their comfort zone. Not to be confused with "a dirty coward", someone who will sacrifice their morals and screw over their friends to avoid something difficult. The Cowardly Lion came through for his friends, otherwise he'd be the Dirty Cowardly Lion. You get it?

Few cowards can pinpoint the moment they became cowards. But I'm in therapy, so I'm real insightful about myself. I had this epiphany in therapy when we were discussing sixth grade. My therapist says a lot of people have epiphanies while discussing sixth grade. A "crucial time in our adolescence" apparently.

Riding four-wheelers is a normal part of life in rural West Virginia. If you're not familiar, I'm referring to "All-Terrain Vehicles", or "ATVs." They're essentially motorcycles with four wheels, hence the nickname. Four-wheelers can't be used on the main roads, but there are plenty of backroads and mud pits, places where speed limits don't exist. Go fast and get messy, and don't wear a helmet unless you're a wimp. I never did anything like race or go mud bogging, mostly because I didn't have many friends. Getting muddy by yourself isn't as fun. Might as well just be a pig. But I drove my four-wheeler on our dirt road to visit relatives, go to the barn, or meet up with my dad in the fields. I didn't go joyriding; it was a practical mode of underage transportation. I was no speed demon by any stretch of the imagination.

But one of those rare days where I decided to take a risk would be a day I'd regret. Dad had left the four-wheeler up at a neighbor's house. They were always swapping out vehicles, he probably had the neighbor's tractor or something. Mom stopped there on our way home from school and told me to drive the four-wheeler home for him, and she would follow in the car with my sister. I took off in front of them while my mom stayed parked to have a chat with the neighbors. Just a typical day.

The distance between the two houses is about a quarter of a mile. I was anxious to get there as fast as I could, probably to play video games or raid Nutty Bars from the pantry. So I figured I'd bump myself up to third gear. I didn't have a clear concept of gears and shifting up back then; from what I understood, if you wanted to go faster you had to shift to a higher gear, otherwise the vehicle would explode. I wasn't supposed to go above second gear, but what can I say? I was a twelve-year-old kid who just wanted a taste of danger.

So I clicked up the gear shift with my foot and took off at a nice…I guess twenty-five miles per hour? Maybe not even that fast. But it felt satisfying.

I decided to cut through our front yard, which meant going up a small bank. I could have kept driving twenty more feet to use the flat level driveway, but I didn't want to waste those precious seconds. Plus, it's more fun to go up a hill! A four-wheeler is an "all-terrain vehicle" after all. So I cut left into the yard and kept the handlebars in the "turn left" position to go towards the house. I was apparently going too fast to be turning this sharp, because physics took hold, and I felt the left side wheels come off the ground.

I had time to think to myself, *"Oh crap!"*, during that frozen second where I was lopsided. In my memory, I want to think I tried shifting my weight to the other side. I probably didn't because I wasn't that fast or that smart, but if I did it was all in vain anyway. Time resumed and I felt my body hit the ground as the bike continued falling. All of a sudden I was on the grass, with my legs pinned underneath the four-wheeler. The handlebars pressed painfully into my left leg. The engine purred above my head as I lay there, pinned down in my own front yard.

Before I continue, let me remind you that I was twelve. At twelve you're smaller than most people and the world is a big scary place. I remember watching a particular episode of that TV show, *Rescue 911*. I watched, in horror, a grainy reenactment of a child getting his shoelaces stuck in an escalator and then slowly being pulled under the toothed platform at the top, and that image has stuck with me for years. Every time I would see an escalator afterwards, I thought of that poor kid. Statistically it's highly unlikely that you would get stuck in an escalator, but you don't know statistics at such a young age. So now I always have a firm grip on the handrails and carefully watch my feet the entire ride to avoid the teeth at the end.

I also remember, as a kid, watching news stories on TV before my sitcoms started. Stories about serial killers or home invaders still on the loose. With no grasp of the difference between "local" and "national" news, I'd think all the serial murderers were running around my town. I'd lock the front door every night, even though we lived in such a rural area where locking doors was considered silly and unnecessary.

My point is that things at that age appeared bigger and scarier than they really were. Looking back on it, I was obviously fine. Sure, there was a four-wheeler pinning me down, but there were no bone breaks or bleeding. But when I looked behind myself, all I could see was a big ol' four-wheeler on top of me. It was a bit terrifying; I was used to it being the other way around!

So I started screaming "Help!" And crying. I kept that up for a few minutes but then had to stop: yelling is exhausting! I knew Mom and my sister would be along eventually. But what if Mom remembered she had to go back to town for something? I could sit there for hours. Thoughts like that didn't soothe my panicked brain. It was very overwhelming: there was the physical pain, the shock, the fear that I was going to get in trouble for driving too fast, the betrayal that this stupid machine had turned on me.

For a few moments I just lied there, trapped under my four-wheeler, and looked out at the farmland in front of me. The land I saw every single day but never really took the time to *look at*. It was like sitting on a porch swing, except I was the swing and a small motor vehicle was me.

Eventually my mom and sister pulled up. Mom was out of the car right away and by my side; I resumed crying. "I'm sorry" I kept saying over and over again through my tears. Victims often blame themselves. I was hurt but I also felt like I'd done something wrong. I was speeding, after all. Mom was alarmed but handled herself well. Not knowing how to get the damn thing off me, she pulled out her newly purchased cell phone. She told me she was going to call 911.

"Oh wow, 911." I thought. This was getting serious. Was I going to get in legal trouble now? I was technically below the age of operation limit on the four-wheeler. That's two of many laws in West Virginia that no one abides: be a certain age to drive a four-wheeler and always wear a helmet. Am I going to be arrested? Will my parents be arrested for allowing me to drive this? Are we going to go to prison as a family except for my sister, who will then have to go into foster care? Is this going to end up as a reenactment on *Rescue 911*? I wanted to say "we don't need to call 911" but on the other hand, my leg *did* hurt.

A few minutes later Dad showed up. Mom had apparently called him before or after calling for an ambulance. I can't be sure: do you call the other parent or the paramedics first? Whatever answer *you* think is most responsible, that's what we'll go with. He ran over and lifted the bike off my leg without thinking twice about it. I know…I'm also disappointed that my mother didn't do that first. You hear those stories about moms getting superhuman strength and picking flipped cars off their children. All my mom had to do was lift a four-wheeler, considerably lighter than a car. Sure, she knew I wasn't dying, she could see the top half of me. Maybe if there had been blood, she could've picked it up and thrown it across the yard, and we could've made the newspaper. I'll give her the benefit of the doubt.

I felt the four-wheeler come off my legs and both me and my legs were relieved. Then I heard Mom yelling at Dad, "Don't drop it on him!" Wait, what? Dad could *drop* it on me? Well that would suck. I resumed panicking. Looking up and seeing my dad's face as he held up the bike, I'd like to say that I was confident he wouldn't drop it on me, the firstborn son. But uh…well. His face was scrunched up like he was struggling, and Ma had already suggested he could drop it. Dad didn't lift weights or vehicles for a living, he drove a truck. How far could I really trust this man? So, like a fat shabby Army recruit in a movie, I pushed myself forward using my arms and cleared my body out from underneath the four-wheeler. Seeing that I had moved out of the way, my dad gently put it back down. We all played a part in getting me out.

Except for my sister. She just cried in the car the whole time.

At some point someone must have uttered, "Well, it can't get any worse, can it?" because it started to rain. A nice strong sprinkle was in full effect by the time the ambulance showed up. The paramedics started asking Mom all the required questions. They noted that I wasn't wearing a helmet (whoops!), that I was not sixteen, or thirteen, or whatever age was deemed acceptable. Could I move my leg? I wasn't sure, I was afraid to try. They decided a trip to the emergency room was in order.

If you've ever been loaded into an ambulance, then you know they put you on a stretcher first. The stretcher was a thin yellow plastic thing, like a child's sled, and it made me nervous. I was a slightly bigger kid, and it was raining, and my leg hurt. Did I have to go on this slippery stretcher? I made scared noises and worried faces and Mom asked the paramedics not to put me on the stretcher. They complied and brought the gurney bed out into the rain and loaded me directly onto it. I know, I was such a difficult customer! I tipped them twenty percent when it was over, so it's cool.

I shouldn't write off riding in an ambulance as a boring experience, even though mine kind of was. It's not like the scenes on TV, there were no tubes going into my face or anyone yelling "Clear!" But it was probably a good thing my ambulance ride was boring; a boring ambulance ride is preferable to an exciting ambulance ride. I just had a little bit of pain and a lot of fear, lying in this little white room on wheels. I remember liking that the siren was on and knowing that we'd get to go through red lights. People were stopping on the streets *for me*. Sure, they didn't know it was for me but that's got to count for something: I stopped traffic.

While being taken into the emergency room I heard a flurry of questions and answers orbiting around me. There was a lot of repetition: "You didn't use a stretcher?" "No, patient's mother refused it." Well, that's pretty emasculating, I'm right here, you guys. I also kept hearing the phrase "patient was not wearing a helmet, patient was not wearing a helmet." And I get it, the doctors have to say this, and you legally do need to wear a helmet. I'm a huge supporter of wearing helmets, don't get me wrong, and think it should be mandatory, especially if you ride a motorcycle. As Mom likes to say, "I don't give a shit if you die on a motorcycle, just wear a helmet so I don't have to look at your brains splattered across the road." If nothing else, you should wear a helmet to be considerate of *others*. "Patient was not wearing a helmet." I understand that, you're a doctor and you have a checklist to go through with everyone to make sure no one dies. But in this case, my head was fine! How about we focus the attention to my leg?

My brief stay at the hospital only lasted a few hours but felt like forever. I waited while they asked me questions, then they took X-rays. At one point I peed myself because I was too scared to say anything to anyone. They gave me a set of hospital pajama pants, the kind that have no business feeling as comfortable as they do. All this waiting and humiliation to be told I should stay off it for a few days, but that otherwise I was fine.

But I wasn't fine, I was unwell in a way no one could see. Sure, they didn't take x-rays and say, "Hey, your leg is fine, but did you know about all these tumors?" My leg wasn't broken but my head was shaken. I'd experienced danger and faced mortality, and a fear had been planted. I wasn't someone who got a rush from the adrenaline, who would begin chasing after dangerous scenarios to capture "that feeling." I left the hospital with a pair of crutches, new pajama pants and some brand-new anxieties.

There's that old adage that says, "If you fall off the horse, you gotta get right back on." But that was never me. After my spill I started to notice the dangers around me. For starters, I realized how certain machines or vehicles were more prone to tipping than others. On West Virginia farms you'll often see tractors driving along the side of a hill. Does no one else understand this? These tractors are riding sideways on *hills*! Accidents are rare, but they do happen. And that thought was all it took to keep my chest in knots while my dad mowed the hayfields.

I would refuse any time Dad asked me to take the four-wheeler somewhere. If I had to go to the barn to feed my 4-H calf, I'd just walk. It wasn't that far. But my dad didn't see the logic in it; the four-wheeler was clearly much faster. "Never walk somewhere when you can ride somewhere." Which probably meant, "You're on a farm so you're going to be tired enough without all this extra walking." But in my opinion that stance seemed a little anti-exercise.

For a few months I refused to drive a four-wheeler. Not on the gravel road, not on the hills, wouldn't drive it anywhere. I didn't trust it not to turn on me again. I could tell some of the time it would frustrate my parents, but they wouldn't press the issue too much. They figured I'd eventually have to "get back on the horse", as the saying goes.

I don't know how anyone can be thrown off a horse and then get back on top of it. Where does that level of trust come from? I didn't trust this four-wheeler anymore, and it was an inanimate object. An inanimate object that had betrayed me. I'd lost my confidence in being able to drive. I'd lost my confidence for a lot of things.

Over those next few years of childhood, I became well associated with Fear. I didn't want to go rollerblading out of fear of falling down. I wouldn't dive off the pool diving board because I was worried I'd hit the bottom and split my head open. I didn't want to go on roller coasters because I was worried the bars wouldn't latch and I'd go flying into the air after the first drop. Fear had moved in and made itself quite comfortable.

Learning to drive a car was an ordeal. I was a nervous Nellie behind the wheel, and my poor mom lost her patience many a time while she was "teaching" me. I'd wrecked a four-wheeler going 20 miles per hour; now I was in a much larger metal container going 70 on the interstate. While, at the same time, hundreds of other people were doing the exact same thing. It's insane! How could anyone keep calm doing that? I didn't see cars; I saw potential accidents. I didn't see a fun horse ride; I saw broken limbs and necks. You couldn't trust anything not to hurt you, be it vehicle, animal, or person.

I wasn't a brave teenager either, if you were expecting me to suddenly grow out of it in high school. Didn't do sports, didn't misbehave much. Football? Broken bones and head injuries, no thank you. Underage drinking? With my luck I'd be in an accident, killed, and then somehow arrested. Dating? No. That could only lead to heartache, which would lead to depression, which could lead to suicide. I had to play it safe.

I wrapped myself up in a cocoon of my own making to avoid any pain. Nothing could hurt me if I didn't take any risks. Nowadays I wonder if I missed out on anything in my youth. Maybe I should have skipped class that one time to go smoke with my alleged friends. I could have driven more places, gone to more parties, really cut loose. Lived a little. Alas, I didn't. I stayed home. I played it safe. A coward. A wimp. A pussy.

Because, see, living on a farm and being afraid of machines and animals makes you a joke. People notice you refusing to participate, then dub you a waste of space. What's worse is you start to believe it yourself.

Eventually through necessity I *did* have to get back on the four-wheeler. I don't remember why, but time was of the essence, so I had no alternative. I didn't flip it over on myself that time.

That, of course, planted the seed in my head that I'd be okay. I started driving it again when I needed to get somewhere. I was still scared of driving it on hilly areas covered in mud, but I could at least drive *to* the hilly areas covered in mud.

But given the option I'd still rather walk. There are more health benefits to walking. No one ever said, "Hey, nice ass! You must drive a lot of four-wheelers."

But the truth is, I don't have an epic hero story for you. I didn't face a mugger in my twenties and come out on the other end a stronger person. I didn't jump out of an airplane and have some sort of epiphany as I free-fell through the clouds. I still have fantasies about how I could be a badass like in the movies. Shoot down all my enemies, rob a bank, spend the money on cocaine and prostitutes. Stand up to my demons, literally sucker punch the Devil himself.

I don't think those stories are common. I became a coward. But I kept going. I live with my fear. I don't have PTSD, I just constantly worry about the things to come. What *could* go wrong, what bad things *could* happen. Worrying about pain before having to feel it.

But I've been able to conquer fear in other ways. I moved away after college, left the same zip code that I grew up in. And it wasn't a slight against my family or anything, I just wanted to see more of the world. Live in a place totally unlike the only one I'd known. A lot of my friends just stayed put, had a few babies. Perhaps they're happier like that, I shouldn't judge. But I think some of them were just afraid to take those risks.

And I failed a lot. That's one good thing about fear; it prepares you to face failure. And everyone experiences failure, that's just part of living. It's how we deal with them that shapes who we are. As a kid pinned under a four-wheeler I had a crash-course (do you get it?) in fear and failure. Things don't always go the way you expect. You may be a coward, but you don't have to always be afraid.

Dispatches from a High School Band Fag

<u>Freshman Year</u>

-Today is the first day of Band Camp. It's not an actual "Camp", like a bunch of kids living in cabins for a month playing their instruments all day. Band Camp just refers to a week of practices before the first day of high school. During this week we'll learn the halftime show, start memorizing music, and get to know each other. We start at eight in the morning and we're there until eight at night. I'm a little nervous. I liked playing saxophone in middle school, but marching band never appealed to me. I've never been a "sports kid." But, "You need to do *something*," my parents said, "You have to have some extracurricular activity. You can't just do nothing." I like playing video games but apparently that doesn't count. There have to be other *humans* involved in my extracurricular activities. It felt too late to learn a new sport. But I like playing music, so marching band seemed to be my best bet. I think it'll be okay.

-We start the day with exercises, to warm up and work on marching drills before the sun comes all the way up. It's too early to make conversation, and I don't really know anybody so I don't want to talk anyway. I stretch and do pushups and run laps around the field with the rest of them. After a few laps I'm already sweaty and puffy, and I'm not the only one. It's kind of embarrassing when we run laps. In other athletics all the players are in shape. In band a lot of us are on the heavier side. If marching band is a sport, it's one that you can do and still be fat. Like bowling.

-Dad was late in dropping me off today and I got in trouble, I guess. If anyone's late we all have to run extra laps, but I walked up just before eight. The older kids told me to "Run!" but I wouldn't; we have running to do later. They were pissed off at my attitude. It was pretty embarrassing; I had no idea we were taking it this seriously. Guess I sure learned my lesson! "Don't be late for band camp, this is serious!"

-The other saxophone players are nice enough. We've bonded a little during sectionals time. I think I hate the senior class, as a whole. They seem grumpy. They act like they're better than me, which I have to agree with: They're older and they've been doing this longer. They don't have to go out of their way to feel superior. My current strategy is to just keep my head down, memorize my music, stay on the right foot, and try to blend in. I've been doing okay so far.

-This has been much more exercise than I'm used to. Warming up gets me sweaty, and running drills keep us on our feet for hours. It's exhausting. The heat doesn't help either. I've gotten the expected tan line from my sax's neck strap. The rest of my neck is sunburned, so the strap rubs the burn when I try to move it. "Band camp isn't for wimps!" is what the instructors say as they fan themselves, standing stationary in the shade while watching us march. I don't think I'm a wimp, per se. I think I'm just sweaty and have a sunburn. I'm uncomfortable.

-Lunch is good.

-I've never heard of these songs we're playing. I didn't realize how limited my exposure to music has been. My parents have kept the car radio on the same two country music stations my whole life. Never once did they flip over to pop music or even oldies. And now I look stupid because I don't know the music of Journey, or Queen, or Tower of Power. Not that it matters anyway. When you're playing the second alto sax part you're playing the most boring harmonies on the field. Sometimes you wind up playing the same three notes over and over again for an entire song. Brass instruments get all the fun melodies because they're naturally louder. They say every part is important on the field, but no one ever sings along with the harmonies.

-Learning spots on the field is quite the process. You're given a dot book that you use to keep track of your moves. You write things like, "By the time you're playing measure 32 you should be 6 steps to the left of the right 40-yard line." But you don't actually write that out, you do it with pictures and stuff, it's hard to explain. It's also boring, so count yourself lucky if you don't know what I'm talking about. It's nice to see I'm not the only one struggling with this. However, I do memorize my music at a quick pace (those same three notes are easy to remember) so I can devote most of my brainpower to remembering where I need to march to. There's such a feeling of relief when we all hit the picture at the right time. Usually someone messes it up and the director yells, "Go back and do it again!" We do that a lot.

-Band camp ended today. I think everyone's glad it's over. I know I am. It's been a pretty long week. There was some freshmen "hazing" on the last day. Nothing horrible. You just had to stand up in front of the whole band and shout this dumb pseudo-sexual phrase at everyone. But I couldn't do it. They tried to force me, but I refused and wouldn't let myself be dragged up onto that chair. I couldn't face those kids that yelled at me just a few days ago. I think now they like me even less for not doing it. I feel like I've humiliated myself a lot this week. I kinda want to quit, throw my dot book in the trash, and run as far away as I can. But my parents would never go for that. My calves are too sore for more running anyway.

-High school is weird. And big. And a little chaotic. I don't have a lot of classes with my old friends from middle school. Usually I just glance people I used to hang out with in the hallways, and I'll get a quick wave out as they rush by. A lot of my fellow "band kids" are in my classes, though. Not those intimidating upperclassmen who screamed at me, but the kids in my year. I've been sitting with them at lunch too, since all my old friends aren't in my lunch period either. Yep...I'm at the band table now. I don't talk a lot there. But they don't seem to mind me and let me eat my grilled cheese in peace.

-Tonight was the first home football game. My family keeps asking me what it felt like being on the field for the first time. I don't know how to answer that. The band uniform is incredibly uncomfortable, especially the stupid top clasp on the jacket. It chafes the front of my neck, which balances out the strap irritation on the back of my neck. The hat pinches my head in a weird way, like it's slowly drilling into my cranium and giving me a premature bald spot. Oh, and the sweating! I was ready to be off the field right after the first drop of sweat crept down my forehead and into my eye. But you have to keep going, you're in it until the end now. Left, right, left, right, get to your spot on time, don't mess up your music, and ignore the stinging wetness in your eye. I reassured my family: "It was so fun!"

-It took a while, but I think I've bonded with a few of the other band freshmen. I speak up more at lunch now and they seem to be amused by my sarcasm. We bond about the mutual classes that we dislike and who in the school annoys us. It's easy to be cynical about everything when you're the "band fags" and are therefore "uncool." I'm now a part of a little circle that forms before practice starts or after games end. I think I'm finally making friends.

-The stand tunes we play are kind of fun. Stand tunes are little songs played during the parts of the game where they reset the players or run the Zamboni or something. Usually they're old rock and roll songs like "Louie, Louie." No one's really paying attention to us when we play them but…it's something to do, I guess.

-Apparently there are marching band *competitions*. Who knew? It's exactly what it sounds like; a series of marching bands performing their halftime shows one after the other and getting scored for it. And at the halfway mark they play a quick 15-minute game of football, har har har. We're not really a medal-winning marching band. We don't even place. Our director seems peeved by that. Everyone else doesn't seem to care much, mostly they're annoyed that they have to spend their Saturday at a marching band competition. It's understandable.

-Some of the other marching bands at that competition were insane. Most bands were kind of like us, sitting in the bleachers and cheering for whoever took home the prize. But these stricter bands even had regimented applause. They would stand up as one, wait to hear the results, and then politely clap in time. I get having discipline or whatever, but wow. This is high school band, not the Queen's Honor Guard.

-Winter is here. These football games are becoming more of a process. Everyone tries to see how many layers we can cram under our already ill-fitting uniforms. We shove Hot Hands™ into our gloves to keep our hands warm. The instruments require extra attention since the cold weather affects the sound quality. It's weird, only a few months ago it was too hot and now it's way too cold. I guess part of marching band is never being comfortable.

-The football team SUCKS. I have no idea why or how because I still don't understand the rules. But we've only won one game all season, so it seems like they suck. From what I've heard, if they were good then that would mean *more* football games, so I suppose it's a blessing that they suck.

-I may not know much about football, but I've enjoyed

making fun of the team with the other saxophones. My friend Alana will constantly gossip about the players. Number 33 is in her science class and always reeks of BO. Number 24 slept with a friend of hers and he apparently has a weird-shaped dick that he's sensitive about. Number 4 once peed his pants in middle school. Eventually we'll move on to upperclassmen in the band ("Well you know *she's* a slut"), the director ("Clearly not getting any"), the field commander ("Herpes!"). She's very funny. I need the laughs to get through these games sometimes. Ok, all the time. They're so boring.

-I don't want to brag here, but guess what? I have *rhythm*. I know this because I get frustrated at the people who don't. How hard is it? "1, 2, 3, 4, left, right, left, right." It's quite simple. Yet people keep messing it up and we have to drill over and over again. Unnecessary. I can't yell at anyone though. I'm just a Freshman and, as you know, most of them already hate me.

-Football games are over, because the team had bad standings and didn't go to the playoffs or whatever. So that means it's Christmas parade season! Marching in straight lines and playing the same two Christmas tunes over and over for an hour. It's a test of endurance, physically and mentally. Some part of me does find it exhilarating to march through the lit-up streets of town while a light snow falls and people cheer on the sidewalks. It's kind of beautiful. That is until about halfway through the parade, when I feel like vomiting and start wondering how much more of this shit we have to endure.

-We're now preparing for our Christmas concert. I like

concert band better. You get to sit down, and the music is more fun to play. Not that I'm big on Christmas music, but you take what you can get. The saxophone part even gets a little melody now and then, which is like a small Christmas gift. Did you hear me on the "Fa la la la la la la la la la"?

-The second semester is moving quickly. Freshmen have now been assimilated into the ecosystem. Everyone's generally found their groove, and, except for the occasional candy fundraiser, the band doesn't have as much to do. Spring concert band is fun though, the music is more challenging. Although I'd say maybe half the band isn't up to the task. Not many students seem like aspiring musicians. Looks like my parents weren't the only ones who forced their kids into a group sport.

-I am so sick of non-band people quoting that damn movie to me. "So one time, at Band Camp, did you ever…" OH MY GOD SO FUNNY! You're quoting a funny line from a movie in everyday life, you are soooooo funny! I hate that movie. I haven't seen it, but I hate it.

-No one actually physically bullies you for being in band, no "heads in lockers" or anything like that. Mostly if you tell someone that you're in band they just make a confused face and go "…why?" There's no acceptable answer to this. Just shrug and keep going.

-This was our last week before summer break. The seniors had their final day of classes a week ago. It's been pretty swell without them here, I gotta admit. We've been given our sheet music for next year's marching band show. We were advised to start looking at it now, so we're prepared when band camp starts. My friends and I won't look at it until the day before we need it. Happy summer!

<u>Sophomore Year</u>

-Band camp has changed its length this year from being one week to two weeks, but we aren't there all day. We go home at 4. It's basically like a school day, but all the periods are band. It could be worse. Could be a day of all health classes, or trigonometry. Although those classes would at least have air conditioning.

-Some freshman girl almost passed out today while we were running laps. Sounds intense, doesn't it? It's weird; we do all this work: we sweat, get sore, and almost pass out, just to ultimately do a ten-minute show that most people won't see because they're in line for nachos. Seems kinda…not worth it, you know? Anyway, I think that girl had asthma.

-I don't drink Gatorade and I think it's weird that people do. I know it's just as hydrating as water and has good stuff in it, but frankly the lemon-lime color reminds me of a really gross pee and that turns me off. What *is* it anyway? A sports drink. A SPORTS DRINK. A DRINK for SPORTS. It's got stuff in it that helps you play SPORTS.

-There's something to be said about the instrument you play and how it relates to your personality. Woodwinds, the flutes and clarinets, tend to be a bit submissive. A lot of quiet girls in that section. Brass players, trumpets and trombones, are a bit cocky. Definitely the "alphas" of the band, at least in their mind. Tuba players seem to not care much about anything. Drummers are a bit dumb but think they're super cool because they have the big bad drums. Obviously, saxophones are where the real cool people are.

-There's this new guy in the band, in addition to all the new freshmen. He's a year older than I am and he plays the trumpet. He seems pretty cool, kind of different from the other upperclassmen. Like he seems smart but he's not overly obnoxious about it, like most brass players would be. He likes to win arguments, and he often does. I want someone to make him feel stupid once. I also want to be his friend.

-So obviously the point is to get the ball from one end of the field to the other and I think you have to do it in four turns? Or you have four chances to get past a certain line or else the other team gets the ball. The cheerleaders chant, "first and ten" at some point, that's usually a good thing. Cheerleaders, by the way, are never the cliché you think they are. They aren't the popular hot girls, whatever that means. They aren't evil mean girls either. They're…just fine, nice girls.

-It's interesting how much pain people go through for things like this. "Wear sunscreen during band camp, you could get sun poisoning or cancer!" Wouldn't it be easier to simply *not* spend hours marching in the sun? Same thing happens in football; they could get seriously, maybe even permanently, hurt from playing. Why do it? I know; it's the thrill of the game that you're chasing, to hell with the risks. Am I supposed to be chasing some good feeling or adrenaline rush right now?

-I think the hardest part about marching band is pretending to give a shit when a player gets injured. Like I don't want to wish bad on anyone, but he is such a *dick* to me in homeroom and I don't think he'd pretend to care if *I* got hurt.

-There are two kinds of Christmas music: "Ho ho ho" Christmas and "Amen" Christmas. For this year's parade we're doing "Walking in a Winter Wonderland", which is "Ho-ho" Christmas. Some of the parents are upset about it, since it's not a religious Christmas tune. Like we're succumbing to the censorship the liberal agenda is forcing on us and refusing to say the word "Christmas." Our band director has informed us that's not the case. "I just picked a song that I knew you guys could learn easily so you don't look like idiots out there." Merry freaking Christmas.

-I've had a lot of talks with Lance, the new guy trumpet player, about Christmas and religion. Actually, it was more like he talked and I listened. He's an atheist. Isn't that exciting? I never met one before.

-My band friends like to read a lot of manga. Manga is Japanese comic books, in case you don't know. That's how I explained it to my parents anyway. It's different from anime, which is Japanese cartoons. Like *Pokemon*. Some of it's funny but overall, I can't say I love it. But they keep lending me these books and I want to fit in, so I keep reading them. The problem is that comic books never end. If you read one issue, at least ten more follow it. I don't have time for that kind of commitment. I have video games to play.

-I'm in jazz band this spring semester. I thought it would be fun, like a bonus concert band. I like "swinging"; playing jazz, that is. I don't know how I feel about wife-swapping. When you're playing swing you hold some notes slightly longer and play the following note a little faster. It's hard to explain in English, it's more something you just have to feel out. Music is a language, after all. Anyone can learn how to play an instrument, but learning to play music is something special. Like a sixth sense. Jazz is so different from marching band. More loose, more free. More room to be yourself. Jazz, man. *Jaaaazzzzzz.*

-Lance drove me home after jazz practice today. He told me about the Kurt Vonnegut book he's reading (not even assigned reading, he's just reading it for fun!). I didn't quite comprehend it, but it sounded pretty awesome. He also recommended me a manga he says is better than what I've been reading. He's so cool. His parents are divorced.

-Did I mention the band sells chocolate-covered pretzels as a fundraiser? The nice "gourmet" ones. They're no Girl Scout cookies, but they're almost as perfect. It's a deadly flavor combination: a salty crunchy pretzel rod covered with basic milk chocolate. So simple and beautiful. It's like Minimalist art. They're addictive as hell too. I've already spent about $20 just on myself. I have no regrets.

-I have come to the realization that I may be an *actual* band fag. Alana commented that she thought Lance was really cute.

And in that instant, I realized that I totally agreed. Shit. This is kind of scary. I never really thought about it before, but then I always kind of knew? Huh. I guess Alana knows too or else why would she make that comment to me? This is a lot. I think I'll just keep it to myself.

-We're on a band trip to New York City! It's the first time in the "big city" for most of us. I keep tripping on the sidewalk because I'm staring up at the skyscrapers. I feel like such a hillbilly tourist. I think New Yorkers are worried I'm going to spit tobacco on their shoes.

-Went to the top of the Empire State Building. Bunch of long lines full of sweaty tourists. After riding about four or five elevators we got to the top, where we looked down at the sparkling night time of NYC. I'd like to say I enjoyed it, but it was really windy and cold so I went back inside.

-Sleeping arrangements in the hotel are complicated. I wanted to share a bed with Lance but knew our other roommates would give us shit for it. Also…would he even want to? I slept on the floor, like the cool "totally not a band fag" guy that I am. Hyper masculinity is fun. It wasn't that bad. I bought some ibuprofen for my neck.

-The Statue of Liberty looks like every picture of the Statue of Liberty that you've ever seen.

-Saw *Hairspray* on Broadway. Even the kids who are kind of ignorant and homophobic admitted they had a fun time. But then who doesn't love Bruce Vilanch?

-We watched *Saturday Night Live* back at the hotel. I never really watched it before. It was pretty funny. I laid on the bed next to Lance as we watched it. For a brief crazy second I thought about resting my head on his shoulder, just to see what would happen. Instead when *SNL* was over I pounced back to my space on the floor, to once again count the patterned squares in the carpet until I fell asleep.

-Just got off the charter bus. It's nice to be back home again in West Virginia.

-I lied.

<u>Junior Year</u>

-Summer went by way too fast. I can't believe Band Camp is starting up again. I also can't believe how it used to scare me. If anything, it just feels annoying now. There are new freshmen, new songs, new routines, but it's just the same old tedious shit. Listening to our director yell about straight lines and marching on the right foot. Getting dehydrated from spitting into a horn and sweating all day. Picking at sunburns while I lay in bed trying to fall asleep. Having gone through it before I know that the end of the camp always comes and things will be better when practice is over. Why do I still do this when all I do is complain about it? I think these are just my people now.

-God I hate whistles. Is there any sound more obnoxious than a whistle? So shrill and sharp, demanding attention and respect although it has done nothing to deserve it. You play ONE PITCH, whistle, who do you think you are? I could smash you with my saxophone if I wanted to. Aren't coaches obnoxious enough without their precious whistles?

-There's a new girl in the saxophone section this year. Her name is Lyla. I'm pretty sure she was high every single day of camp. We've become fast friends.

-So Lance gave me a ride home after camp. We were having another good talk, although now I can't remember what it was about. As I was saying goodbye, I mustered up some courage and I kissed him on the cheek. I mean I was aiming for his lips but caught his cheek. He was moving around. I was nervous alright? I'm not sure what I thought that would accomplish but I'd been thinking about doing it for months and had to go for it. He looked at me in shock. I looked at him. Then I said, "Thanks again," and jumped out of the car. Actually, I think I tucked and rolled. Or maybe I jumped through the closed window. I don't remember.

-Well, I'm terrified. Just outed myself to my crush, who is probably freaking out right about now or organizing a hate mob. Why did I do it? I don't do bold things. That's not me. I wonder if he'll tell anyone. I don't want this getting out. I shouldn't have done anything. This could be my last post. Tomorrow could be my last day. That sounds a little dramatic. But this *is* Small Town West Virginia, not exactly known for having the backs of queers. I guess we'll see.

-I think I'm okay. Lance gave me a reassuring smile today. A smile that said, *"We're cool"* but we didn't get to talk one-on-one. I think I get to live. It doesn't seem like he's told anyone about it. I'm still embarrassed, but I think my heart is slowing to a normal pace.

-Wow, realizing that you're a band fag really changes your perspective on football. At school these guys are just the mindless dicks with uneven scruff and bad acne. But when the helmets go on they become indiscernible soldiers, working together in manly unity towards the same goal, literally. It's not as beautiful as making music, but I respect them for their teamwork and endurance. Plus, I've gotten good at spotting the outline of a jockstrap.

-Homecoming weekend is coming up. I don't like dances, with their stupid songs and the crowning of the Queen. What a dumb thing. Does anyone actually *want* to do these things, or are we just told to look forward to it? I mean I see my friends at school every day; why do we have to hang out in the gym and pretend to like the rest of the student body? It's ridiculous. I'm sick of this school-sanctioned crap, what is the point? "Homecoming." What does that even mean? We already live here; we aren't coming home. None of this makes any damn sense.

-Lance invited me to join him and some other friends in their group for Homecoming. We both agree it'll be lame. But, hey, there are worse ways to spend an evening. I'm not a hypocrite. Shut up.

-I wonder if I'll ever know the lyrics to "Hang On Sloopy."

-Homecoming actually ended up being more fun than I would've guessed. Our friends snuck booze in, I had a little but didn't get drunk. Lance stayed sober so he could drive everyone home or whatever place they were taking their post-dance festivities. Eventually it was just the two of us in the car. Lance started talking about colleges he was looking at and how the future was a big unknown where anything could happen. I was a little tipsy at that point, so he was kind of hard to follow. I heard something about "discovering ourselves" or "listening to instincts." Maybe I was drunk after all. Before I knew it, his lips were all over mine. It got a little dangerous because I forgot to make myself breathe. I'm not sure how long it took me to catch my breath. Actually, I'll let you know when it happens.

-Just once I'd love it if the announcer asked, "Are you all ready for some football?!?!?!?", and the crowd yelled back, "NO!!" and went home. Come on. That'd be hilarious. Senior prank?

-Have I ever mentioned our band uniform has white shoes? WHITE shoes. That we have to clean and polish before competitions so we don't appear sloppy. What kind of monster makes white shoes for anyone, let alone a marching band? We walk on asphalt, fake turf, real turf, mud, dirt, the occasional snowy slush. In *white* shoes. We have polish we put on to clean them up, but we need something stronger. Like lead paint.

-Neither Lance nor I want to deal with the unwanted attention of being the "out and proud" gay couple at school, so we're keeping things under wraps. Also Lance says he's bisexual, which is a tricky concept to explain to kids that have the Confederate flag painted on their trucks. So…it's like dating but it's not. Just hanging out in public and making out in secret. It's exciting, like a forbidden romance. I'm a woodwind, he's a brass. It's like Romeo and Juliet, except gay and hopefully not a tragedy.

-Lyla told me that the embouchure (mouth shape) required to play the saxophone also works well for giving blowjobs. I think someone should put that in a pamphlet about why band is cool.

-Concert band season again! It's strange how much I look forward to it and jazz band. Making music is so much better without the marching. Making music because *you want* to make it. It's not for the football team or the crowd; it's for you. People don't come to a football game to see the band; if football didn't exist marching bands would be obsolete. The crowd doesn't respect it. What do the parents or the other students know about music? Marching band isn't pro-music or pro-arts, it's just pro-football. Then the band kids get called "losers." What bullshit. I should start smoking cigarettes with the angry kids behind the school, because life looks really stupid from the band bleachers.

-You know what time signature I love? 6/8 time. Six beats a measure and an eighth note gets one beat. A lot of kids have trouble grasping the concept, but I love it…123, 456, 123, 456…it just flows so nicely. I'm sorry, I guess if you don't know how to read music this doesn't make any sense. If you do know how to read music…well who cares? Moving on.

-Lyla was right about the blowjob thing.

-Lyla is one of the handful of people who know about me

and Lance. We've told a couple of our friends, just the ones who'd guessed it anyway. It's still kind of a secret, but I'm sure the majority of the band knows anyway. Secrets are like currency here. Band fags like to gossip you know.

-Have started playing cards with my friends during lunch, mostly Euchre. A lot of the redneck tables also play Euchre during lunch. It's one of those rare things that kids from different backgrounds have in common. We have fun and it makes the day move faster. I never win though.

-Band is a sort of a family. Even the people you hate you feel a kinship with. Although we're not all technically fags, I like to think we're all band fags. I think instead of trying to fight back and prove to the world we aren't, we should just embrace it. Really own it, wear t-shirts that say, "BAND FAG AND PROUD."

<u>Senior Year</u>

-Today is a beautiful day: it's my last first day of band camp. Ever. When it's all over, no more being out on a hot field or teaching freshmen how to march. I have four more months of mandatory football left. After that I never have to watch it again. I mean…that's awesome, right? Who knows what I'll be doing at this time next year? It could be anything. It could be nothing.

-It's easier going through band camp with three years under your belt. Things aren't scary anymore. The freshmen seem so little and timid. Only three years ago that was me. Was I this quiet? That seems like a different lifetime. I'm trying my hardest not to act like the seniors I had to deal with when I was a freshman. I'm trying to be friendly and supportive. I try to make things fun at band camp; there's enough yelling coming from the instructors and the Field Commander. You can take things seriously and still have fun.

-At the end of last spring I tried out for Field Commander. I don't know why, I thought it would be fun to conduct the band. Perhaps I was just chasing an ego trip or something, wanted to be seen at the head of the band. Thankfully, though, I sucked and didn't get it, so I'm just head of the saxophones because I'm the only senior. Probably a good thing I didn't get it. I'm better at supplying much-needed sarcasm as opposed to giving commands.

-Just a brief update on Lance: he's gone off to college in Indiana. We ended our "hidden" relationship amicably. Neither of us really wanted to deal with keeping long-distance going. It hurt a bit during the summer, but I know we both have different lives to live. He couldn't wait to move away and neither can I. We still text now and then.

-I haven't taken the time to look up the song "25 or 6 to 4" but I now have the marching band version memorized. What does it even mean? Is it like "9 to 5" but a longer day? I wake up at 6 and school lets out at 3:30 so I guess that makes sense. Still, what's this 25 about? The seventies were so stupid, it's probably just a drug reference. It all comes back to drugs.

-It was Senior Night at the game. That's when seniors on the football team, cheerleaders, and band get "honored" for their last year. The honor is that they read your name and a bio of your accomplishments out loud during halftime and people clap. But all we'll ever remember is how much it *rained*. Rained and rained and rained. Not enough to cancel the game of course, but just enough to make the field a disgusting mud bowl. We chose, as a senior class, to do the traditional walk down the 50-yard line with our parents. One by one we held onto our drenched parents as we slopped through the muddy field with heads bowed low. This was *our* time, damn it, and we weren't going to waste it. It sucked, but we didn't have to do a halftime show so it's a win in my book. I think it would've been more enjoyable had my socks not been wet.

-We competed in our final band competition today. After four years I actually started to care a little bit. This year when we lost horribly, I was kind of bummed about it. But on the bus ride home I got over it. Over the years it feels like we've all grown individually as people, but as a marching band we've pretty much stayed stagnant. We're not the underdogs in these competitions; we're the feral cats you don't let in the house. I guarantee I'll never see another marching band competition in my life. Unless I have a child. But my kid won't be in band.

-I skipped homecoming. I know, *"You didn't go to Homecoming on your senior year?!?"* No. No, I did not. I just didn't feel like it. It's not like I had a date, and if I did I wouldn't have been allowed to slow dance with him anyway. So no, I didn't feel like getting dressed up and acting like any of my years here will have any significance on the rest of my life. I stayed in. I played video games alone. And I don't really regret it.

-I've been clinking around a bit on piano lately. I'm not a great player but I'm having fun learning it. I only bring it up because I've learned how to play "Linus and Lucy." It's an annoying song because it goes on in a loop forever, but damn is it fun to play. Plus it's like a Christmas song that's not about Christmas, so everyone loves it.

-It's Christmas and all I want from Santa is to charge through the next few months and graduate. I'm tired of this town, I'm tired of these people, I'm tired of this band. I mean I love my friends and I'll miss them. But at the same time moving forward sounds wonderful. I thought I wanted to keep studying music after high school, but I don't even know anymore. I like making music in a group, but something just seems…flat. The music I'm making doesn't *mean* anything to me. No one seems to care. Maybe I'll join a garage punk band. I might have to play something besides saxophone.

-New Year, new me? I'm so close. So close to whatever the hell happens after high school.

-Started looking at colleges. Well, starting to look at colleges I've been told we can afford. Which gives me about 2 options: Big University or Little University. Big University is further away so I'm leaning more towards them. My parents are pushing for Big University: "You can be in their marching band too!" I'm sorry, what? I don't even know what I want to major in yet.

Perhaps they can also decide that for me. When's the part where I get to make my own choices?

-When I started sharing these dispatches I was talking about band stuff, and now I'm just whining about my life. I'm sorry. Let's see, band stuff…um, I broke a reed today and it pissed me off. And it was the last one I had so I have to buy a new box and they're not cheap. It's not as interesting anymore, is it?

-I've been told my attitude lately is "senioritis", referring to the feeling most high school seniors get that's basically, "Fuck it, I'm out of here soon anyway." I get it. Can you blame us? We've been here for four years, we were in school for nine years before that, and all anyone talks about is where we should go to school for four *more* years. It's exhausting! I'm tired! I don't know what I want to do next week, and people are asking what I want to do for the rest of my life. I almost sympathize with those asshole seniors from when I was a freshman. I think I finally understand where the bitterness came from.

-The band trip this year was to Chicago. It was an awesome time. We saw *Wicked* and ate deep dish pizza and looked at the bluest water I've ever seen. I thought about getting "lost" and not getting back on the bus. But I didn't…I'm back here in West Virginia. The river seems browner than usual.

-Every high schooler and parent says this, I know, but graduation gowns are a fucking racket. I don't even want to walk at graduation but, you know, "YOU HAVE TO!" Just another one of those fucking things you have to do. You have to buy the gown, you have to walk, you have to go to prom, and now finally you're an "adult." As an adult you'll have to spend money on things people tell you you'll need, like a graduation gown or health insurance. People like to say that "real life" sucks and school is the best time of your life. I don't know how, because if I had to do one more year of high school, I'd lose my mind. Bring it on, "real life."

-Graduation day. We threw our hats up in the air anyway, even though they told us not to. We don't give a fuck.

-Well, my time in high school has come to an end, so this is my last post. I'm not telling you what I'm doing after this. Maybe I'm going to Big University, where I'll march in the Big Marching Band and write new dispatches about that. Maybe I'll head to Little University and become a pothead Philosophy major. I may run off to Indiana to see Lance. Or I could run away to Chicago and just start fresh. Maybe I'll just do nothing for a while, become a homo hobo. Band was with me the whole time, for better or worse. When I started the band, I was a shy quiet kid who was afraid of everyone. Sometimes I still feel like that kid. But I think ultimately band changed me for the better. Made me outspoken, gave me confidence, maybe made me a little bitter. I never did lose weight in marching season, but that's between me and Pop Tarts. I still love music. Whether or not I keep my saxophone or never pick it up again, I'll remember the times I was making music.

Manson Wanted to
Live Here

Hello hello! It's nice to meet y'all. Not many people these days moving *into* the state. Just call me the "welcome wagon." The community got wind that someone was moving into this house from out of state. So we gave you a few days to settle in and now that it looks like you are, I thought I'd come introduce myself and give you a tour of the town. If that's okay with you all. It is? Great.

Now before we go through the town, what do you all actually know about the state of West Virginia? I'm sure you've done a little research before deciding to move here. I know there's not a whole lot of common knowledge out there. Heck, most folks don't even know we're a state. When we say "West Virginia" they say, "Oh, which part of Virginia?" I bet the whole West Coast don't even know we exist. Isn't that incredible? It's like we're forgotten land or something. It's exciting to see that people like you are moving here.

Of course, the most popular stories from here tend to be our bad stories. People always think of those feudin' hillbilly families, the Hatfields and the McCoys. Or that *Wonderful Whites of West Virginia* documentary. Or the banjo-playing albinos from *Deliverance*, and you know that story took place in Georgia? I'll be honest with you; we get a bad reputation from the rest of the country. Too many people mock our state without ever having been here for even a visit.

But those stereotypes aren't the West Virginia we know and love. Not enough gets said about the real community here, the great unspoken bond that connects us. It's a state filled with good, hard-working people who are always ready and willing to help someone in need. Folks around here have strong hearts and are smarter than they get credit for. But the ignorant outsiders like to focus on those headlines you read online, like "Number One in Obesity" or "Growing Heroin Epidemic." Those are problems, of course, I'll be honest with you. But there is so much to appreciate in this state, probably too much to list, really.

So how about it? Anyone know any "fun facts"? Yes? That's right, the state bird is the cardinal, beautiful birds. What's that? Yep, black bear is the state animal. You did some research on Wikipedia, didn't you? I've lived here all my life and never saw a black bear in the wild. Guess I'm thankful for that, huh? Alright, how about the state motto? Don't know it? "Montani semper liberi," which is Latin for "Mountaineers are always free." Don't feel bad, not many people remember that one.

If you know one thing about this state's history, then it's probably about the coal mining that we're so famous for. There aren't many active coal mines left around this part of the state, you'll have to go further south to see 'em. You can take a guided tour through some of the old ones that aren't in operation anymore. Lots of history in coal and West Virginia, that's for sure. The Coal Wars were a big deal here, and a lot of people still remember them. You don't forget things like that.

Ooh, have y'all had pepperoni rolls before? They're our local delicacy, I guess. Back when the coal mines were active, they employed a lot of Italian immigrants. Their wives would bake pepperoni and cheese inside of bread dough and pack it up for their lunch. The grease in the pepperoni makes the bread hard, so it holds up well even while you work underground for hours. And now people make them for any occasion: football games, family gatherings, what have you. They even sell them for school fundraisers. It's not a very complicated dish, but hey, it's the little things, right? It's funny that some parts of the country have never even heard of 'em.

Now you've already driven through the state to get here, so I don't need to tell you all about the rolling hills with the beautiful forests and rivers. God's land, isn't it? Wait 'til fall when the leaves have changed colors. Beautiful. It's even pretty in the winter when everything's covered in that crisp clean snow. Just make sure you keep your eyes on the roads; they get icy. No matter what season it is you'll always have some beautiful land to look at.

What's that? Oh, yeah, sure there have been a few gas wells built in the last couple of years. That's caused a bit of controversy, I'll be honest. But I don't think fracking's really as bad as people make it out to be. You hardly notice them after a while. Just be careful driving the backroads, you'll likely get stuck behind one or two of their big trucks.

My point is, you've seen the land already. So why don't I take you through town?

Our first stop is the Mound here. Big, isn't it? Waaaay back before civilization started this land was inhabited by a people known as the "Adenas." They would build giant mounds like this one as burial grounds to honor their dead. When their most-respected warriors or tribe members passed away, they'd be buried inside these mounds along with some of their possessions. I guess in their culture, you *can* take it with you when you go, huh?

Only a few of these mounds are around today, but this one here is the largest of what's left. Remember, folks, this was built entirely by hand. They didn't have any machinery or anything else like that to help them. There were no blueprints either, it's like they just somehow knew what they were doing. Gotta admit, they did a real good job. It's what they're most remembered for, and it's been standing here well over a hundred years.

What? No, we can't go inside it unfortunately. It's sealed off now. Architects cleaned it out a long time ago. But if you ever want to see what was there, the artifacts are on display there across the street in that little museum. Well, no, it's closed at the moment. No, they don't have the bones of the people there. Ain't you morbid? But it is a neat thing to go look at if you ever have the time. And on a nice day the Mound is the perfect place for a picnic.

Now you can't miss it, of course, but there across the street is the famed Penitentiary. Kinda makes the Mound look small, don't it? Oh the stories I could tell you about the old' Pen. There've been quite a few books written about it. The Mound may be our oldest landmark, but the Pen is what put us on the map. Now you should definitely take the full tour sometime and get a more thorough rundown, but for now I'll just tell you what I can recollect.

The Pen was the prison for the whole state back around the 1870's. Shortly after West Virginia became a state, the folks in charge got to thinking they had a need for a giant prison. It was gonna be unlike any prison anyone had ever seen before. The "Taj Mahal" of incarceration. The people in charge had to pick between two options for where to build it: either here or a town further downstate. Obviously, they decided on here. That other town became home to the state's University.

Yep, I'm sure you've heard all about Morgantown. It's a big college town, isn't it? The kids here that get into college often go there, and kids from other states flock to it too. Although I don't know if it's always for educational purposes. "The number one party school in the country," they say. Some might think we were dealt the losing hand, having this big prison built here instead of the University. After all, the University led to Morgantown becoming huge. It's one of the most populated cities in the state now, and we're still on the smaller side. It's quieter here, that's for sure. The Pen may be a bit creepy, but it gives us our own little charm. I surely wouldn't want to switch places.

After a while the Pen started to get a bad reputation, even by prison standards. It became overcrowded, with three or four men living in a tiny cell at once. It was torture for them to live like that. Then there's the punishments they were given, which actually *were* torture. I mean, really, the devices they used to punish prisoners looked like they came out of a medieval times dungeon. It's hard to believe how they were treated back then, total disregard for human life just because they were incarcerated.

Back in those early days the Pen held public executions. This was back when they hanged people you see. That big archway there? That's where they'd do 'em. The bodies would drop down from that little door there, and spectators would gather here below. One time there was a bit of a "snafu" and the rope wound up decapitating some poor bastard. Took his head clean off and scared the crap out of all the onlookers. After that, hangings weren't public anymore. Sorry if that was too graphic for y'all.

As the times changed executions were switched from hanging to electric chair. The one in the Pen hasn't been fired up for years, obviously, but you can still see it inside when you take the tour. "Old Sparky." I know, is there an electric chair anywhere that *isn't* called "Old Sparky"?

Some of you may think it's strange having a prison so close to this residential area. A lot of folks found it a little unsettling. I mean if you think your last neighbors were annoying, imagine living next to a castle full of prisoners! It sounds scarier than it really was, though. Some folks remember hearing all the inmates hooting and hollering at midnight on New Year's Eve. Isn't that something? Trapped in such horrible conditions and still celebrating the New Year. Amazing how people can look on the bright side of any bleak situation.

Take a moment to appreciate the beauty of this building. The architect sure had a field day with it, didn't he? Those high walls, the turrets, the coils of barbed wire on the fence. It looks like Frankenstein's monster could come barreling out the front doors at any time, doesn't it? Yep, this place is the only thing in town that can be called "Gothic" that isn't a high school sophomore. That's a little joke my son made up for me.

But really, you should take the proper tour sometime. If you grew up here, you'd have been taken here on a field trip. Yeah, the kids love it. Sometimes they make them all stand in the cells and then they close the gates on them for a laugh. Always gives 'em a good scare. Some of the kids cry, but most of them laugh.

Oh, that across the street? That's the roller rink. Yeah, a lot of kids' birthday parties are held there. It's a fun time.

Anyway, back to the giant prison. On the tour you'll see all the important rooms: the mess hall, the big courtyard, the many cell blocks. There's all this graffiti all over the walls: cryptic messages, screaming skeletal faces, monsters. I'm not sure if the prisoners did it or if teens put it there after it closed, but either way it's really neat to look at. There's some scary stuff in there.

Now I'm sure you've heard it's haunted, right? The town's really gained a lot of popularity with our "haunted prison." Everyone says it's haunted, even people that aren't that superstitious. A lot of paranormal researchers have come here to study it and we've been featured on a few ghost-hunting TV shows too. The general consensus is that because so many people were executed or murdered here that there are a lot of angry spirits trapped in those walls. If you believe in that sort of thing. Which most people here do.

According to these researchers the most haunted area in the prison is "The Sugar Shack." That was the activity room where the inmates would go to hang out, play some cards, and get a little "sugar," if you know what I mean. It was the most dangerous place to be, full of fighting, murder, rape. So it stands to reason that it's the most haunted room. Some teenagers like to dare each other to spend the night in the Sugar Shack. Allegedly you'll start to hear screaming so horrible that you'll never be able to close your eyes, let alone sleep there. It's a scary dare; I've never done it.

Anyway, in October they turn the prison into a real haunted house for Halloween, and boy is that popular. People from all over the Ohio Valley come in to walk through it. They work hard at putting it together. There's mazes, trapped rooms, people jumping out at you with chainsaws. No better way to spend a Halloween, right? People really love it.

Oh! We even made it into a video game! My son told me the Pen inspired a "haunted prison" level of this zombie game. *Left 4 Dead* I think it's called. We've never had an Oscar-winning film or anything made here, but we made it into a video game. That's pretty cool, right?

One last thing about the prison: It's got a bit of a celebrity endorsement. On display in one of the rooms is a letter written by the late Charles Manson. He had family in the area and, while he was incarcerated, he wrote a letter requesting to be transferred to the Pen. His request was denied, but still: flattering, isn't it? Charles Manson wanted to live here! That's crazy!

Well anyway, the Pen was shut down and a new prison was built on the outskirts of town. Yeah, it's near the fairgrounds. It's not much to look at, compared to the Pen. It's more practical; just a place to keep the murderers and druggies. There are signs around it that say "Beware of Hitchhikers" in case someone breaks out. Oh, but don't worry, that hardly ever happens.

I'd show you the fairgrounds but there's not much to see at the moment. In July, the barns are full of animals, the rides are set up, all the food stands line the street. It's a fun time, everyone loves the fair. But for now, let's look around the rest of the town.

Now one of the biggest changes that's happened in the last twenty years or so is that right there: the Walmart Supercenter. They took this big empty space right in the middle of town, leveled it out, and put up this Walmart. People were really excited about it. The grand opening was an event, the high school band performed and everything.

Walmart changed a lot of things. Teens started hanging out there after school like it was a youth center or something; they roam the aisles or just hang out in the parking lot. It brought new jobs to the town, but it took some away. See that big empty building next to it? That used to be the main grocery store before Walmart showed up. It closed a little while after Walmart opened. Just couldn't compete. Walmart has more affordable food, and you can buy clothes and electronics there too. I guess you just gotta give the people what they want.

The rest of this little shopping center has formed around the Walmart. First Walmart was here, then they added a Burger King. Then that gas station. Then that Buffalo Wild Wings, then that hotel over there. As you can see, more things are being built and I'm not real sure what they're gonna be. Amazing, isn't it? Watching a town grow before your very eyes.

Now if you're hungry you can find the standard fare of restaurants here. For fast food, there's a McDonald's, Wendy's, the Long John Silver's just reopened again. We used to have a combo KFC/Taco Bell, but they split up a few years ago. Now there's just the KFC and the Taco Bell is right across the street. The Pizza Hut is there, but the health department shut it down again. They get put under new management a lot.

But honestly, if you're looking for good pizza, check out this place here. It's a unique style of pizza. They bake the sauce and dough in the oven by themselves and then throw the cheese and other toppings on top cold afterwards. I know it sounds strange, but it's honestly so delicious. The crust is all crispy and the cheese is only half-melted, my mouth is watering just thinking about it. Everyone around here loves it; they got a few locations throughout the Ohio Valley and people will fight about which one is the best. You have to get it with the extra cheese, though, take my word for it.

There are a few diners here and there, some of the bars have decent food menus. We also got two Chinese food buffets, if that interests you. Most people prefer one to the other, but I'll let you make up your own mind. Personally, I think the food is better at China Garden, but they speak better English at China Wall so…yeah, I'll let you make up your mind. There's also two Mexican restaurants, but you definitely want to go to the one on the main drag. The one on First keeps getting shut down. Drug busts, that's the rumor anyway.

A lot of the small businesses are here on Second street. The banks are here, a few stores, the old toy museum, barber shops. There's the theater. It used to be a theater for plays, then it just showed movies, and then it was closed for a long time. But in the last few years the community theater folks got it opened back up again, so they can stop doing plays in the high school's auditorium. It's really nice in there, you should check out a show sometime. Last summer they did *Grease.*

Now just look at that right there. Is that not the nicest high school football stadium you've ever seen? Yeah, that was built a couple of years ago, but they keep it shiny and clean. Got that new scoreboard that even does instant replays. You go to some of those away games in Ohio and they just have a row of bleachers in a muddy field. Barely even have a sound system. Here you get the whole experience. Friday night football is a big deal around here, and I hear the team's pretty good this year.

That used to be the drive-in. I know, pretty rare to see a drive-in movie theater in this day and age. It did pretty good business in the summers, but the owners sold the space to the gas people to park their trailers and mining equipment and what not. So: no more drive-in. If you wanna see a movie you can either drive over the bridge to the mall in Ohio or drive over to the big shopping center off the highway. It's about a thirty-minute drive either way.

An old buddy of mine once said this is such a great town to live in, because it has everything you'd ever need. I like his love for our little town, but if I'm being honest you will have to do a bit of driving if you want to go see a concert or something like that. Pittsburgh isn't *that* far away, really. But aside from that, I think everything you need is right here.

Although if you want a good cup of coffee you may have to go out for it, I'll be honest. Mostly gas stations and fast food options around here. Some people think it's snobby of me to tell people this, but I get it. Once you've tasted good coffee it's hard to go back to whatever comes out of those machines at the Exxon station.

Now if it's not too personal, what religion are you all? I'm sorry if that's inappropriate, just wanted to make sure we can get you all set up with the right church. We've got a lot in town, ranging from Methodist to Catholic. Oh, not really "church people" huh? Well, that's fine too. Though it is a good way to meet people in town. Even if you don't belong to a denomination, you should introduce yourself whenever there's a spaghetti dinner or the like going on.

Jewish? Well, that's nice.

You see this big empty field right here? This used to be the Fostoria. It was a giant factory that made glass products for the whole country. It was finally sold and shut down in the eighties.

The factory stood empty for years after that. It was massive. After years of no one caring for it, the place started to fall apart. Broken windows, crumbling walls, garbage all over the grounds. It was impressive once, but it became a real eyesore.

Well just last year they finally demolished the damn thing. Tore it down, not a trace of it left. Just this big empty field. I know it doesn't look like much now, but fear not, something great's gonna go here one day. I have a good feeling about that. The last empty space we had in town got that Walmart and look at all the good that's come from that! Things are really looking up for this little town. You should feel lucky, this is such an exciting time to move here.

Does Not Count

As a child Billy liked chasing after cows. He knew he wasn't supposed to, but it gave him such a rush. Dad would tell him to stop running at them; it made them panic and that made it harder to get them going in the direction you wanted. Cows weren't supposed to go outside the fence, and nothing made Dad more upset than when they got out. Billy wondered why the cows always became excited when they saw a hole in the fence. They had such a seemingly good life: troughs full of water, fields to run around on, salt blocks to lick. His parents used his puzzlement as a way of teaching him that old analogy, "The grass is always greener on the other side."

As Billy got older Dad would swear at the cows in front of him. Billy was in awe of his father's ability to effortlessly string cuss words together. He rarely lost his temper, and Billy never knew him to be a violent man. But after so many minutes wasted chasing cows, he would start to lose patience. Then every swear word you could imagine would come pouring out of his mouth, like a man possessed by demons or diagnosed with Tourette's. It was still English: direct objects, adjectives, nouns, verbs, and so on. It didn't make much sense though, but maybe in Dad's mind it did. Perhaps he was a poet in that way. Billy's jaw dropped the first time he'd heard it.

Nowadays he had to work hard not to laugh while it was

happening; he thought Dad would prefer if he pretended not to notice. No one likes being laughed at when they're angry. Some days after chores and homework were finished, Billy would try to watch *The Simpsons* on TV in the living room. "Turn that off, it's trash." Mom would say, cracking open a Diet Coke. Billy wondered if she'd ever heard her husband yell at farm animals, because there were words in the fields that Billy had *never* heard on TV before.

Their farm wasn't a large operation, but it kept Dad busy, and Billy helped out when he could. Animals needed tended to, fields needed plowed, hay needed baled, fences needed mended. Billy hated fixing fence the most, such a tedious task. There was always something. His parents insisted he keep up on his schoolwork too. There was no excuse for bad grades or being lazy with the farm work. Of course, Dad barely graduated high school, but Billy knew better than to use that as an argument. Wasn't worth the fight.

Like most teenagers, Billy looked forward to his summers. Unlike most teenagers, Billy still had work to do, but he relished his long summer days. He'd work with Dad for the majority of the day, taking care of whatever was on the chore list. Sometimes for "lunch break" he'd take a dip in the creek near the woods. When all his chores were done, he'd usually head back to the house to sit on the porch and read. Billy read a lot of books, on account of the television only got two channels. There were only so many sitcom reruns he could watch until getting bored out of his skull. He'd read 'til dinner, maybe watch a little TV with the family afterwards if he was feeling sociable (or if *Survivor* was on). On the weekends or occasionally during the week he'd hang out with his friends, go see a movie or something. Then repeat it all again the next day. There were never any magical adventures, but it was peaceful.

On the last day of Billy's junior year, Dad informed him that things were going to be different this summer. Dad was going to take on some extra help. An old friend of his had a son Billy's age. This friend was going away on a long trip with his wife for the summer ("A well-deserved second honeymoon, probably the second time he's done anything nice for her," according to Mom). Their son wasn't a child, but his parents didn't feel comfortable leaving him alone for the summer, didn't trust that he would do anything useful with his time in their absence. So, a deal was made: this boy would stay with Billy's family for the summer and assist in the farm work, in exchange for food and shelter. The boy would also be rooming with Billy.

Billy started to protest but he was pleading to deaf ears, as usual. His dad reminded Billy that he would also benefit from the extra help around the farm; he'd have a little more free time. Mom had said it would do him some good to make another friend. But Billy *had* friends. Mom had met those friends. But she always said he could have more if he were a little more outgoing. He didn't need more, and he definitely did not want to share his room.

He'd had a bad enough time the summer of the two-week summer camp. He'd hated it, unlike his little brother Denny who went every year. Sleeping in those weird little cabins with those bunk beds full of other boys had been a rough two weeks. They made noises all night, snored and farted and yakked. Night was the one time Billy was able to read but sharing a cabin of twenty had made that difficult. It was kind of nice to be off the farm, but Billy preferred being left alone. He'd rather do farm chores all summer and have a room to himself.

He also hated the way that camp made you line up before lunch. It's lunch: Just sit down and eat.

But it had already been decided. Billy was gonna have a roommate. His name was Jacob.

Jacob's family lived a county over, so he didn't go to Billy's high school. They'd never met, but Billy could tell what kind of guy he was the moment their car pulled up. Blonde and fit, the athletic type. Football in the fall, track in the summer. Could just tell by his face he probably didn't get good grades, had that kinda smug look that comes with being able to glide through life. Of course, Mom was smitten the moment Jacob greeted her with a smile. She always said she liked dimples on a man, despite the fact none of the men in her family had any. Dad was greeted with a firm and confident handshake. Billy shook the new boy's hand halfheartedly and answered his, "How's it going, man?" with a mumbled, "I'm good."

After visiting a bit and then saying goodbye to Jacob's

parents, Billy showed Jacob to their room. He'd just cleaned it that morning at his mom's insistence, not that a teenage boy would be judgmental about another teenage boy's cleanliness. He watched as Jacob scanned the room, taking in the full bookshelf against the wall and the old but comfortable folding bed that Dad had dug up for him.

"I'm sorry about this, man," he said as he laid his bags down. His voice was deep but nonthreatening. "I'm sure you're pissed having to share your room with someone all summer." Billy shrugged politely, pretending that he didn't find the entire situation inconvenient. "My parents are so annoying. They think I'll do a bunch of wild shit or something if they leave me alone." Jacob stared bitterly at the wall.

Billy sat down on his bed and gestured around at the room. "Well, they've sent you to the right place: no wild shit to get into here." The dimples reappeared as a dry smile formed on Jacob's face. "What, you don't have hootenannies out here in the Sticks?" He made eye contact with Billy. It was an insult, but it was in good fun. Teasing. Billy's friends made similar cracks about where he lived, usually when they had to give him a ride home. No one liked to drive out Billy's way.

"Afraid not, it's... pretty quiet here." That was an understatement, but probably best to start off easy. He should have made a joke back; why did he answer him like it was a real question?

Jacob nodded, looking out their bedroom window at the

setting sun. "S'kinda nice though. Living in town can get noisy sometimes."

Billy heard shit like that once or twice before. "*Oh, I bet it's cool living on a farm, so peaceful.*" But they'd never trade places with Billy given the option. They were being polite, or they were intrigued by a lifestyle they'd never lived. Billy, on the other hand, wondered what it was like to grow up never having once shoveled shit.

"So what do we like...*do* all day?" Jacob asked, eyeing Billy's full bookshelf a little warily. He probably wasn't much of a reader. "Dad comes up with a list of stuff to do every day. It's usually just a few hours of stuff in the morning, it's rarely like a full day of work." Billy was trying to lessen the blow. It really wouldn't be more time-demanding than your average part-time job, just perhaps a bit more physical. Not that Jacob should have issues with that, considering how athletic he seemed.

Jacob nodded at his reflection in Billy's mirror. He fidgeted a bit with his shaggy blonde hair.

"That's cool. But like, what do you do for fun around here?"

Billy's face flushed a bit as he subconsciously glanced at his bookshelf again. How to answer *that* question...

"Well, whatever we want, I guess. There's always something to get into." Billy didn't sound convincing even to himself.

Jacob looked over at him expectedly, waiting for examples of the fun to be had. Billy kept the eye contact for a moment before looking down at the carpet, embarrassed to be caught in his bluff.

"I read a lot." he admitted.

Jacob looked back at his reflection and sighed a little. "Cool."

There were some kids that would call Billy a redneck. That never bothered him much though. He lived in the right location, sure, but he didn't fit in with the rednecks at school. He lived on a farm and did farm work but didn't look like all the camo- and Carhartt- wearing guys. One foot in that culture, one foot out.

And what did those other kids know anyway? They were just trash from town. That was all his high school was made up of: rednecks and white trash. There are differences, but you have to really immerse yourself to spot them. The variables are how much money you have, how you judge people who are different from you, how many kids you have, where you live in relation to paved roads, etc. Rednecks live out on farms or in rural areas, have an abundance of off-road vehicles, wear camouflage, almost always a hat. White trash live in shitty houses or trailer parks, have neck tattoos, and dress like "thugs." There are assholes on both sides, but Billy believed that belonging to either group didn't mean you were inherently bad. Rednecks and white trash could be good people, like *The Beverly Hillbillies* and *Roseanne* taught us. Billy liked to think his family fell on the nicer side of rednecks. He guessed maybe Jacob's family fell on the nicer side of trash.

Dinner that evening played out like a police interrogation,

but with both of Billy's parents playing the good cop. They fell into a pattern of volleying questions at Jacob throughout the meal, one asking a new question while the other took the time to chew. Jacob fielded them all politely: he was on the football team (of course!), didn't have a serious girlfriend, hadn't had a summer job before, didn't know what he was going to do about college yet. Billy was waiting for his mother to say something like, "Well you're doing better than *Billy* here," but she was too enthralled with the new boy to remember to taunt her son.

Billy was content to just sit in silence and listen to Jacob get the third degree, while Denny sat next to him playing his Gameboy under the table. Usually, Ma wouldn't tolerate video games at dinner, but she probably didn't want Jacob to see her yelling at her sons on his first day in the house. As a subtle punishment, she made Denny do the dishes afterwards even though it was Billy's turn.

Jacob joined the family in watching evening TV. Billy was embarrassed at his family's TV options; cable was impossible to get this far away from town and Dad was too stubborn to get a satellite dish. Jacob smiled politely when Dad told him they all liked to watch *Survivor* together. How freaking corny.

Jacob sat with them and watched a full episode of real American people running around on a foreign beach in their swimsuits. If he found it stupid, then he kept it to himself. He was probably already thinking, "Oh shit, what dumb hick family am I shacking up with for a whole summer?"

When the show ended Jacob excused himself to go back to their room. Billy remained in the living room with his parents, watching the army propaganda shows that came on after *Survivor*. *CSI: JAGNCISTDSVU* or something. After a few minutes, Mom turned to him and said in a low voice, "Why don't you go hangout with Jacob?"

Billy held back an eye roll. "Why don't we just let him get settled?"

Mom leaned in, never one to back down easily. "Well, don't you think he would get settled easier if you were more friendly with him?"

"No, not really."

Mom scoffed and turned back to the TV. "Brat." She muttered. Billy stuck his tongue out at her and they both pretended he didn't really want to flip her the bird.

At about 10:30 Dad decided it was bedtime. "Got to get up and show Jacob the ropes tomorrow." Billy slunk off to his room. His room with someone already in it, in his space. Jacob was sitting on his bed listening to music with headphones. He nodded a greeting as Billy walked in.

Billy took his pajamas into the bathroom, where he brushed his teeth and changed in privacy. When he came back he went straight to his bed and started reading. Mom's command echoed in his head; should he make conversation with Jacob? Might look forced, insincere. Awkward. What would he even say? He tried to focus on his book, convinced himself the other boy was content listening to his music.

The stillness was broken when Jacob stood up, took out his headphones, stripped off his t-shirt and got under his covers.

"Well. Goodnight." He said as he turned to face the wall.

"Night." Billy replied. He put a bookmark in and turned off the lamp.

For not being a farm boy, Jacob quickly began to flourish. He listened as Billy explained all the daily chores and caught on quickly. His natural athleticism meant he didn't tire out, just needed a few sips of water now and then. He showed no distaste for shoveling cow shit and extreme patience when dealing with Billy's dad. Whenever farm machinery would break down, Billy would usually assist his dad by staying silent and passing him tools. Jacob liked to ask questions and engage the old man in conversation, expressed an interest in how the machine worked. If nothing else, he was proving himself to be a good farm worker. Of course, his only competition was Billy, so the bar was set kind of low.

They were winding down while filling up the cows' watering troughs, their last task of the day. Dad had gone back to the house to clean up before dinner. He told Billy to show Jacob how to water the cows, so Billy sarcastically showed Jacob how to turn the valve on and, when the troughs were full, turn the valve off again. Jacob gave a good laugh and turned to watch the cows, seemingly intrigued by them. He asked Billy if he could climb over the fence and pet them.

"You could try," Billy answered, "They're a bit more tolerant when they're eating and drinking. But these cows are pretty skittish. They'll let Dad go near them and some of them don't mind me. But if one starts running then they'll all start running, and if you scare them away while they're drinking Dad probably won't appreciate that."

Jacob chuckled. "Fair enough. They're skittish, huh? So cow tipping-"

"A myth," Billy interrupted. "They're heavy animals with legs. A group of people could probably push one over, but it wouldn't just tip over. Also, it'd be mean."

Jacob shrugged his shoulders and then nodded in agreement. Billy watched him watching the cows, realizing this was probably the closest he'd ever been to livestock. To Billy it was old hat. On elementary school field trips, a teacher would inevitably say, "Ooh look at the cows!" as the bus passed a pasture. Billy and a few other farm kids would look and say, "Yup. So?"

"Look at that little one!" Jacob perked up, pointing at a very fresh calf probably birthed just a week or two ago. She trotted around her mother, who was waiting patiently for her turn at the troughs. Still small, with dark tan fur that would turn black as she grew. So pleased to see this new world she'd just entered, an enviable amount of excitement for life. Jacob probably would have preferred working on a pot farm with undergrads for the "life experience", but maybe cute calves were a nice runner-up prize.

After the troughs were full they walked back to the house in comfortable silence, Jacob watching the cows that started to mosey parallel to them on the other side of the fence. They would be heading to their usual night spot. Habitual creatures, followed the same paths. Consistent and reliable.

Mom served them dinner at the table again. Usually with everyone's different schedules they didn't eat dinner as a family often, so to do it two nights in a row was a rare occasion. Mom was trying to act like they always ate together to impress Jacob. She'd probably give up on this ruse by the end of the week.

The conversation wasn't as inquisitive as it had been the night before, Ma just mostly asked about Jacob's first day on the farm and Jacob continued to answer politely. Billy ate his cheeseburger macaroni and green beans in silence, pleased that Ma had roasted fresh crisp beans instead of boiling up a mushy can.

After dinner Billy went to the front porch to read. After what felt like a half hour later, Jacob came out in a pair of running shorts and a shirt with the sleeves cut off.

"You want to go for a run?"

Billy looked up from his book and met his gaze. He was serious.

"Um. No?"

Jacob laughed as Ma's voice rang out from inside. "Billy! Go with him so he doesn't get lost! You could use the exercise anyway!"

Billy felt his face getting hot as he placed his bookmark and went inside to change.

Billy hated running. He was slightly chubby, not in the best shape, and he didn't have a lot of endurance. Plus, he sweated easily, as slightly chubby people are prone to doing. His feet and thighs would hurt for days after this, he could just tell. He wished his dinner had digested a bit more before they'd started, he could feel a cramp starting to form. He shouldn't have had that second helping.

On top of it all he was trailing behind an athlete. Jacob was the fittest person Billy had ever been in contact with. Running along the beach on *Survivor* was one thing, but when a clean cut of abs is staring at you in your own room it's a little intimidating. Billy had never hated his body until Jacob moved in. Arms, legs, stomach, butt…who knew they could look like that? They had…what was the word? "Tone"? It probably wouldn't hurt for Billy to get rid of his "baby fat," a cute term you use when you are fat at seventeen.

After only five minutes Billy's lungs had burst into flames and sweat was pouring down his back. He could tell Jacob was running at a slower pace so that he could keep up. If he was annoyed about it, he kept it to himself. Billy would get the occasional whiff of Jacob's body spray. That stuff was overwhelming when he sprayed it on in their bedroom, Billy couldn't believe he could still smell it hours later and *outside*.

Why did jocks love that stuff so much, what was wrong with deodorant?

It felt like ages before Jacob decided to turn around and lead them back to the house. Billy's calves were already painfully tight, and they throbbed in anticipation of getting to rest again. His eyes watered and he fought back his urge to throw up. He must have looked pathetic because when they got back to the porch, Jacob turned and said, "Woah, you okay?"

Billy nodded that he was fine as he bent over, trying to catch his breath, hoping he wouldn't vomit. Jacob went in and got them some water. It was the best water Billy had ever tasted. Jacob sat down next to him on the steps and sipped his own glass of good country water.

"Just you wait," he said, "by the end of the summer I'll be a real farmer and you'll be a marathon runner."

Billy cocked an eyebrow and looked at the other boy with a dubious expression. Jacob laughed. The dimples appeared again. "Or, you know…whatever."

It only took about a week until Jacob decided to peruse Billy's bookshelf. Billy cringed a bit when he got to the sci-fi/fantasy shelf. Surely those looked the dorkiest of the dorkiest, but then what did a "cool" book look like anyway?

Those books looked silly, with their glossy covers of attractive men and women wielding big swords or laser guns, but Billy did love them. The idea of a story taking place in a world so unlike the real one enticed him. His mom never understood;

space travel wasn't real, aliens weren't real, so why would you want to hear a story about them? How many *Little House on the Prairie* rip-offs could one woman read in her lifetime?

Jacob had pulled something off from the fantasy shelf. It was the first in a fairly straightforward sword-and-shield series. An impossibly ripped blonde man in a loincloth was on the cover, waving a bloody sword above his head. It looked goofy and the plot wasn't anything out of this world, but Billy had a certain affinity for it. It was a good fantasy story for the non-fantasy reader.

"This guy is shredded," Jacob joked, tapping the cover with his finger while flipping through the pages. Billy flushed at the implication that he read the book just for the guy on the cover. "The covers are pretty dramatic, it's so people pick up the book." Billy explained, noting that in this case the cover had done its job. Jacob was scanning a few pages. "But it's pretty good?" Billy answered in the affirmative.

Jacob sat down on his foldout bed and looked again at the cover. "Do you mind if I borrow it?"

Billy shrugged, trying to mask his surprise. "Sure, go for it." He just encouraged a jock to read, what kind of Breakfast Club shit was this? He'll probably hate the book, but he gets credit for trying. People never borrowed books from Billy. Remembering that, he reached into his nightstand drawer and fished out a bookmark. He held it out in front of Jacob.

"Um, could you just use a bookmark? I hate dog-eared

pages."

Jacob laughed gently and took the bookmark. "You're the boss."

Billy's parents left him and Jacob alone the evening they drove Denny to his annual two-week summer camp. Camp always fell at just the right time, about when Billy would get tired of his brother being around. Always helped him to have that two-week break without fighting over the bathroom or whose turn it was to do the dishes. His parents wouldn't get back until late, so Billy and Jacob had the house to themselves. The boys watched the dust cloud trail after the family car as they left. As soon as it was out of sight, Jacob turned to Billy with that dimpled grin.

"So…do you wanna smoke weed?"

Billy had never smoked before, but he wasn't afraid to. He just insisted they smoke about a hundred feet behind the house and leave no traces of it behind and burn their clothes afterward so his mom wouldn't be able to smell it. But other than that, he was cool.

He kept telling himself he was cool as Jacob showed him how to hold the bowl and how to inhale. This façade fell away a little as Billy had a thirty second coughing fit, while Jacob laughed his ass off. It was so thick in his lungs and throat Billy didn't think he'd ever stop hacking. He thought it stank horribly too, but he wasn't about to talk like a dork in front of Jacob.

An hour later they were lying in front of the TV, heavily

invested in a *Simpsons* episode. Jacob was laughing hard at all the jokes while Billy sat there, just transfixed at the screen. His arms felt like they were asleep. His head was fuzzy, like he was super tired but also too wound up to go to sleep. He was feeling very talkative, yet it was taking him longer to find his words.

"I can't believe my mom is so against this show. Like it's genuinely funny, god forbid we watch something funny in this house." Somewhere else in the room, Jacob laughed and nodded along.

"She's so strict about "trash tv" man, like it's ridiculous." Billy kept going, "I'm almost eighteen, her other son plays *Grand Theft Auto* all day, but, oh, if a TV show makes a sexual reference, clutch the pearls! Like you've heard my dad swear by now, does she honestly think we're going to hear anything worse than that?"

"Maybe she doesn't know he swears." Jacob offered, grinning.

"Ohhhhh she *knows*." Billy shouted (why was he shouting?). "She knows everything that goes on around here."

Jacob was stifling some giggles now. Billy turned his head sharply. "What?"

"Just, uh, getting some stuff off your chest tonight?" still chuckling, the dimples prominent on his face. His eyes were squinty and his face was flushed.

"Yeah!" Billy shouted dramatically. He then started laughing too. "Ohh, is this what pot is?"

"Yeah, its number one effect is it makes you bitch about your parents."

"Let's have more!"

They had more. At some point Billy stopped being chatty and let his mind start wandering. What would life be like if Dad ever bought a satellite dish? The world doesn't revolve around TV, but TV could bring the outside world in once in a while. As a kid Billy was always frustrated at his friends' references to shows he wasn't able to watch. He didn't get the "cool" Nickelodeon and Disney cartoons, he had to settle with whatever sitcoms were on CBS. Nowadays Billy just felt more behind than everyone. There were things happening all over the world that he knew nothing about, and part of the reason was simply that he only had two TV channels to pick from.

"Are you okay?"

Jacob was suddenly sitting down on the floor beside him, looking confused and concerned. Billy stammered a bit, unable to find his words.

"You keep drifting off and making sad faces and it's really weird. Stop it." Billy nodded. There was something calming about Jacob's face, even though his eyes were glossy and a little bloodshot. His smile was reassuring and, as he turned back to the TV, Billy couldn't recall what he was just stressing about.

When the theme song played over the end credits the boys stayed seated on the floor. The usual block of sitcom reruns began. Billy found them a lot cleverer and funnier when he was high. Who knew? Jacob shuffled around all night, laughing at the TV or refilling their glasses of water. Billy felt like a dumb child that needed to be taken care of. He thought he should be insulted, but on the other hand it *was* kind of nice.

Jacob led them to their room after the eleven o'clock news came on. "Your folks'll be home soon, and they shouldn't see you like this." Billy's vision felt a little blurry and he moved like a zombie. Jacob chuckled and leaned in with a wide grin. "They'll think I'm a bad influence on you."

Billy laughed at that, probably because the pot told him to. He'd been drunk with his friends a few times, but this was fun in a whole new way. "No, man, no," he heard himself saying, "This was so FUN. I was worried when you got here that you'd be such an asshole, but, no, you're great."

Jacob laughed as he gently settled Billy into his bed. "Thanks." Looking down at him, Jacob quickly took his pointer finger and flicked it across Billy's nose. "You're great too." They both giggled through their noses. Jacob stripped off his shirt and jeans and plopped into his rollaway bed. He'd politely refused to take Denny's room for these two camp weeks because, even by teenage boy standards, it was pretty disgusting. Billy thought to himself, as the pot helpfully guided him to sleep, how he was pleased Jacob was staying in his room. He eventually nodded off to the sound of Jacob's soft snores.

It happened without warning one night. Billy had considered the possibility of it happening, but after the first few weeks the thought had left his mind. Like they'd made some sort of unspoken agreement.

The farm work had wrapped up early, so Billy went out with some of his friends to see a movie. He'd invited Jacob to come along, thinking his friends might like hanging out with a jock for once. But the other boy declined, making some little joke that Billy probably wanted a break from him at this point. It felt like Jacob was the one who'd wanted some time alone. Billy supposed that was reasonable and tried not to feel insulted by it.

It had been a fun evening, the movie was great, and his friends hit up the only late-night diner in town to talk about it and eat mediocre burgers. The movie wasn't getting as much press as the big superhero blockbuster that came out the week before, but Billy thought it was much better. Of course, his friends had various opinions on that, and they playfully argued about the merits and shortcomings of each film on the drive home.

He was feeling very energized when his friends dropped him off at the farm. He gave them a parting middle finger as they joked about leaving before the Hill People came to kill them. With a spring in his step, he entered the house and said hello to his parents, who were watching the news with neutral expressions. They asked about the movie, feigning interest and getting the title wrong, and Billy happily reported it was great. They nodded approvingly and Billy left to go up to his room.

The door was unlocked, and it was his room, so he barged

right in. The light from the hallway poured in behind him and illuminated the dark room. Before he could turn the lights on, he was able to make out Jacob on Billy's bed. He was naked, his fist clutching himself in a situation Billy was very familiar with. He jerked in shock when Billy opened the door. Someone yelled "Woah!" It may have been both of them. Billy made a point of covering his eyes and backing out of the room.

He stared at the floor in the hallway for a few minutes. In shock, face red. This was a first; not sharing a room with his own brother meant never walking in on someone jerking off. How did he handle this? What was the next step? What do you say to someone you just caught masturbating on your bed? Maybe you just never speak to them again. But that didn't seem like an option; summer was only half over.

He went to the bathroom, just to kill time. Thinking that he had waited long enough for Jacob to resolve things one way or the other, Billy knocked (too late now) and went back inside. Jacob was back on his rollaway bed, now clad in a pair of white boxer briefs. His face was deep red with embarrassment, and he looked like he had given serious thought about jumping out of the window. Billy uttered a "hey" simply out of courtesy. He got a shaky reply.

"I'm sorry about that man, I just..." he gestured lamely at the bed.

Billy waved a hand, tried to be nonchalant. "It's cool man I get it." They both kind of chuckled a little. Neither of them knew what to say. Jacob quickly got under his covers and turned to face the wall as he slept. Billy tried to read his book but couldn't focus. It was surprising, kind of funny, oddly exciting. Something out of a teen sex comedy movie.

He closed his eyes to fall asleep but couldn't shake the image out of his mind. He found himself opening his eyes to look at the ceiling, and then cheating a glance over at Jacob. Jacob had fallen asleep. Billy closed his eyes again, wondering what he had hoped to see.

Hay season was the middle-late part of summer. Dad mowed the hay and then ran over it with the baler. When that was all over, squared bales of hay were scattered over the fields like a giant Battleship board. In the evening, a few farmer friends of Dad's would come by and assist in putting up the hay.

It was done late in the day because attempting to do it in the daytime sun would almost surely end in someone passing out. Billy and Jacob would load the hay bales onto a trailer being pulled through the fields. When they couldn't stack the hay any higher, they rode back to the barn where they then unloaded the hay for storage. It was the most strenuous job on the farm, and Billy was a little satisfied to see that even Jacob looked wiped out after it was done.

When the night's task was finished Billy and Jacob stood around chatting with Dad and the other farmers. Jacob participated in their bullshitting while Billy stood there silently. It was what he usually did, politely waiting for his informal cue to leave. He was exhausted, eager to get back home to a shower and a long night's sleep.

But tonight, Jacob seemed to have a different idea. Peeling himself away from Dad and the others, Jacob strode over and told Billy they were going to take the four-wheeler back. Jacob would drive; he had really taken to riding four-wheelers this summer. Eager to be gone, Billy agreed.

Billy lightly wrapped his arms around Jacob's stomach as they rode. Fast was the only speed Jacob seemed to know. Billy squeezed a little harder as they turned off the road. They were now riding through the fields; Billy could feel the tall grass lightly smacking against his legs. He tried asking where they were going but couldn't make his voice heard over the scream of the engine. All he could do was hold on and hope Jacob didn't wreck.

When the world stopped shaking and the engine stuttered away into the silent night, Billy realized where they were. Jacob had brought them to the swimming hole. He'd shown it to Jacob once and had told him it was clean enough to drink out of. He then pretended to freak out when Jacob took a drink, told him he'd probably catch dysentery. He thought Jacob was gonna throw up right there.

A swim? Billy thought. He wanted to go for a swim after a night of hard labor? What was it with this guy and exercise?

Jacob saw the look on his face and spoke up. "What, don't you want to cool off after all that work?"

Billy had to admit that a dip might feel very refreshing about now. He felt his nerves spike up as he watched Jacob slip off his sweat-soaked t-shirt. Ever since walking in on him the week before, Billy had been very careful about them not being naked in each other's presence. It was too embarrassing for him, and he assumed Jacob felt the same way.

Embarrassment was apparently not an issue tonight, as Jacob casually tore down his dirty jeans and black briefs. A few stray pieces of hay and dirt stuck to his thighs as he stepped out of them. Catching himself staring, Billy hurried out of his own clothes and tried to ignore his flushing face. He tried not thinking of how fat he must look compared to Jacob, or how much body hair he had, or anything else that may not measure up if they were compared.

When he looked up he was startled to see Jacob openly watching him, hands resting cheekily on his thighs. Through the dim moonlight it felt as if Jacob's eyes were giving his body a once over. Billy could only stare back and choke down any insecurities. Then the blonde boy simply said, "Let's go!" and raced towards the pond.

Energy burst from within Billy as the cold water hit his skin. The insecurity and the weirdness stayed behind on the dry land. They became like children, playing in the water and getting into splash fights, jokingly trying to drown each other. Billy had trouble fighting back as the more muscular boy had him in a headlock and tried to pull him under. Billy kept laughing as he was yanked above and below the water, sputtering and gasping for breath against Jacob's chest.

He slipped free of Jacob's hold, but fell under the water. The swimming hole was just deep enough to be scary. Water went up his nose and he opened his mouth from the shock of it. He exhaled out bubbles and panicked when there was no air to take in. He felt Jacob's hands move to under his armpits and, as quick as he'd fallen in, he was pulled back above the water.

Jacob looked half amused and half alarmed. "Shit, you alright?"

Just their heads were bobbing above the water. Billy began to tread water, but Jacob's hands still supported him. Billy managed to nod while coughing and spitting up what remained.

"I'm okay." He meant it. Jacob still held on to him, grinning. The dimples were so close to him Billy could make them out through the darkness.

"Good." Jacob's lips closed the distance, and then not even the moonlight could fit between them.

Billy wrapped his arms around Jacob's shoulders, both of them now supporting the other. They clumsily kicked towards the edge of the pond. As soon as he could feel the muddy earth squish between his toes, Billy planted his feet and kissed Jacob harder. Everything he'd been having trouble thinking about suddenly made sense. It was this; he had wanted to do *this* for the last few weeks.

Their hands now found themselves free to explore the

other's body. Billy briefly felt insecure about his body as he learned that Jacob felt as toned and firm as he looked. But Jacob's hands seemed just as eager. His skin shivered under the other boy's touch, up his arm, across a nipple, the outside of his upper thigh. His blood raced as he realized his desire was reciprocated. He wanted Jacob and Jacob wanted him.

Jacob interlaced his fingers with Billy's and led him out of the pond and to the bank. They laid on a dry, clean-ish looking section of grass and continued what they'd been doing. Fingers and lips and tongues touching new places. They barely spoke, let their bodies communicate for them. Billy wasn't sure he was doing it right but heard no complaints.

Neither of them was prepared to go "all the way" that night. The idea of "being the girl" was scary and more vulnerable than they wanted. Thankfully, there was no need; they were happy enough to be doing what they were. It went on for what felt like a while, until at last their grunting, gasping releases echoed out into the night sky.

They rode back home on the four-wheeler shortly after, this time Billy buried his face in Jacob's neck. He could still smell the stink of the lake and the sweat and the hay on him, and it was oddly the greatest smell ever. Billy's parents had already gone to bed, so they crept as quietly as they could into the house and up to their room. They hadn't eaten any dinner that night, but they didn't care.

Billy locked the door behind him. Jacob was crawling into

Billy's bed, brushing pieces of grass and dirt off his body as he stripped. He slid over to make room for Billy. After his own clothes were thrown to the floor, Billy crawled into bed and snuggled into the blonde boy's arm. He wanted to stay up and talk to Jacob but he also felt like he could pass out right away. He had so much he wanted to say, to talk about, but he also just wanted to keep quiet, enjoy this moment.

He felt Jacob's lips press against his forehead. Somewhere in the dark of his bedroom, he heard a soft whisper.

"Goodnight."

Jacob's eyes got wide at the idea of Billy being the one to suggest cardio after dinner. The initial shock turned into a face of concern. "What?" he asked. Billy shrugged casually, "I thought we could go for a run in the woods." A knowing smile crept on Jacob's face. He nodded, cheeks reddening a bit, "Oh yeah sure, let's go."

Billy liked to think his running had improved this summer. Jacob had taken to running at his full speed, leaving Billy to choke on his dust. But Billy didn't tire out like he used to and thought that maybe he'd even dropped some of that baby fat.

It got darker as they ran, but Billy could always make out the outline of Jacob in front of him. His bare back was glistening with sweat and Billy watched the muscles expand and contract as he breathed. He desperately wanted to catch up to him, get closer, but he still wasn't fast enough. He felt like one of those horses chasing the carrot on a stick.

Jacob slowed up near a larger tree fairly deep in the woods. It was the usual halfway point on their runs. He took a moment to catch his breath. Billy eased up as well, letting the blood in his head stop pounding for a moment. As he got closer, he drank in the sight of Jacob. His blonde hair was damp with sweat and stuck to the sides of his face. The front of his torso was glistening as well, an overwhelming combination of sweat, abs, and a dusting of light brown hair. Damn. Get this guy on *Survivor*.

Billy refused the water bottle Jacob offered him and went in for a kiss. He was met with a warm reception. Jacob's mouth was still sweet from the glaze on the ham Mom had served for dinner. Jacob even held Billy's head in his hands like the cover of a romance paperback. He was laughing. "Shoulda known when *you* suggested exercise."

"Fuck off."

They stood a moment, looking at each other with arms wrapped around tight. With absolutely no one around they could stand like that. No one there to express scorn or pass judgment. For this small moment, on this tiny, microscopic piece of the Earth, they were themselves.

"You wanna come back next summer?" Billy asked playfully, not sure himself if he was joking.

Jacob laughed at the idea, but not in a cruel way. "What a weird summer. I've shoveled cow shit, I've put up hay, I watched an entire season of *Survivor*. Almost read a book."

"I smoked pot." Billy offered.

"Smoked more than that." Jacob countered suggestively, pulling Billy in for another kiss. They laughed through it, then pulled apart reluctantly. Billy dreaded tomorrow; Jacob's parents were coming back. Summer was ending.

"Back to the real world now, huh?" Billy fought hard against his watering eyes. Jacob looked at him, smiling sadly. The only time he smiled without the dimples. "Yeah," he almost whispered, "I guess so."

"We could hang out sometime," Billy offered, "it's not that far a drive, I could even see a football game if I had to-"

Jacob pulled him close and held him there. He nuzzled Billy's cheek with his nose. Billy let a few tears fall. He absorbed the warmth from Jacob's body, not registering the stickiness from the sweat or the smell of his body odor. The truth was sinking in.

He heard Jacob's voice in his ear, "I had so much fun. Thank you."

As he jogged behind Jacob on the way home, Billy wondered if he'd ever kiss Jacob again. He started to feel sad, but then decided he could do that tomorrow. Tonight, he would keep running behind him.

The old cliché was that you always run into someone you know at Walmart, but Billy wasn't thinking about that as he ran inside. He was just bracing himself to fight off townies for some last-minute Thanksgiving ingredients Ma needed. He did a double take as he rounded the corner into the bread aisle and spotted Jacob.

His hair was cut short and simply, not the long locks he'd had when he stayed with Billy's family all those years ago. It was a little thinner now, but then so was Billy's. He had an unfortunate-looking goatee, but his face was still attractive enough that he could pull it off. Still had those dimples. His body wasn't as tight or as tan anymore. He was still in relatively good shape, just with a slight beer gut now. His eyes lit up when he saw Billy.

They exchanged pleasantries, Jacob grabbing him in an enthusiastic "bro hug." It was friendly and non-suggestive, not at all like the last hug they'd had in the woods. They ran through the usual list of catchups. "How have you been, what are you up to?" They were Facebook friends, of course, but neither of them really posted much.

"I'm just picking up some beer before we head to my in-laws' for the holiday tomorrow."

Ah yes, the wife. Billy knew her from Facebook. Very pretty girl, seemed nice, didn't post much about politics, shared a lot of juvenile memes. Billy hadn't been invited to the wedding, unsurprisingly. She seemed a nice and safe choice. No babies yet, but they had time. They were still young.

"How about you? How long are you in town for?"

"Oh, I took the week to come home." Billy said. "Ma's excited to have the whole family here this week. I'm grabbing some last-minute stuff for her. My boyfriend's waiting in the car, I didn't wanna subject him to Walmart madness."

Jacob nodded enthusiastically. It had been a bit forced, but if he was gonna bring up his wife, then Billy was obligated to mention that he too was in a stable relationship. A relationship that his family had come to accept, over time.

Time stopped for a moment in that Walmart. Billy looked at Jacob and briefly imagined a life where they'd both be going to Billy's parents for Thanksgiving. It would have felt impossible at the time. It didn't seem that impossible now. Whole new world.

Jacob seemed to be remembering things too. Maybe it had been a while since he'd thought of that summer. Billy wondered if he remembered any of the farm labor he'd done, the cows he'd loved to watch. Or reading a book in the summer, or going skinny dipping, or sharing a bed with some nerd who lived on a farm. Billy wondered if Jacob's wife knew his history. Maybe it was a dark secret. Or maybe it wasn't a secret, maybe she knew and it didn't matter in the slightest. Brave new world indeed.

"Well it was really great seeing you, Billy. It's good to see you're doing well."

Jacob went in for another hug and Billy was struck with a strong sensory flashback: *God, did he still wear that same body spray?* Jacob's hand landed gently on Billy's arm as he pulled out of the hug.

"You have a good Thanksgiving."

"Yeah. You too, Jacob."

Billy watched as Jacob turned the corner, to the self-checkout machines and to his normal life.

Ronnie

Helen Maye was putting a can of corn into a cardboard box when she caught a glimpse of herself in the hall mirror. An old woman doing charity work. Her hair was grayed, her skin wrinkled. Her eyes looked tired behind her "old lady glasses," as her grandson liked to call them. When did she get so old? Probably around the time her third grandchild was born. When was the time her hair was long and brown, when she could move gracefully around a room instead of shuffling? A time when she didn't call her left knee her "bad knee"?

Those days were long gone, though. Now she was an old widow going to volunteer at a canned food drive. A woman who went out to dinner at four in the afternoon with other old women from church. No longer did she hang out with friends at her house, listening to records and smoking grass. Really, where *had* the time gone?

She gave the old woman in the mirror a smile. It's not such a bad life, girlie. You've got some great kids, beautiful grandchildren, and you keep yourself busy. You're donating food to the needy. That's admirable; something to be proud of when you go to bed at night. And you don't look bad for…well, however old you are.

After her little pep talk, she went to the "laundry room" to get a coat. It was just a little enclave in the front hallway where her son had moved the washer and dryer into. Her kids had decided she was too old to keep doing her laundry in the basement. Before she grabbed her favorite moss green coat from the hook, she thought to check the washing machine. Damn. When did she put this load in? Was it this morning or yesterday? She made a little note in her head to remind herself to move it to the dryer as soon as she got home.

Back to the kitchen for the box, her bad knee stinging a bit as she walked. She double-checked her daily pill box on the kitchen counter. It was…Tuesday today, right? The compartment with the little "T" on it was empty; she was doing good. She turned back to the table and saw a can of corn sitting out. "Stop it, Ronnie," she mumbled as she put the can back in the box. She braced herself before picking it up. It was heavy, but she could manage it. She wouldn't be put out to pasture just yet. With one last glance at herself in the mirror, she shuffled out the front door to her car.

The gaggle of ladies were fussing about in the church basement when she got there. "Clucking hens" was a rude way of putting it, but Helen thought it appropriate sometimes. One of the younger women tried to take the box from her when she walked in. "Oh Helen, you shouldn't be carrying that. We could've gotten it for you." Helen tightened her grip on the box and insisted she was fine. She put the box down pointedly on the table, ignoring the dull pain in her arms.

She went over to where Ruth was taking inventory. Helen

liked Ruth; she was a little batty but had a boisterous laugh with a good sense of humor. Ruth liked to stay active in her old age. Helen thought by being friends with her that maybe some of that lively energy would rub off. Ruth greeted her with a smile and a sheet of paper to take stock. Helen started going through the closest box and marking what had been donated. She listed a couple boxes of pasta, a few bags of dried beans, some SpaghettiOs. You could tell who had bought things specifically to donate and who just used the drive as an excuse to clean out their cupboard.

"Beets." Ruth said distastefully beside her. "Who donates beets to the needy? Aren't they having a hard enough time?"

Helen smiled. "I like beets, Ruth. And everything helps."

Ruth rolled her eyes playfully. "Well, you're one of the few. I bet you when this is all over we'll have twenty cans of beets left. Oh, and this can of creamed corn."

Helen knew she was right. People clamored over the cans of green beans but avoided the other vegetables. Apparently, beggars could be choosers. Helen was happy not to be the one to watch them get picked up. There were certain rules about how many items someone could take, to keep it fair. But Helen hated policing people. They were hungry, times were hard, and they needed food. It broke her heart to watch. Not to mention the people that came in that were known to be drinking away what little money they earned. The other ladies would utter rude comments about them, but Helen kept her opinions to herself.

The drinkers were struggling too. Obviously if you had money for alcohol then you should have money for food. But Helen knew alcoholism was more complicated than that from helping her daughter get sober. She didn't share this knowledge with the rest of the church.

More women showed up to help. Soon a little circle had formed and they began to chatter about their lives. Whose grandchildren just got their driver's license, if anyone had seen any good movies or read a good book lately, the message of the sermon from last Sunday. Small talk could be tedious, but Helen politely contributed and let herself get lost in the work and the conversation. A few hours of this and the afternoon flew by.

Helen said goodbye to Ruth in the parking lot, reminding her that they were playing Pinochle that weekend. She sat in the front seat of her car and sighed, tired from being on her feet all afternoon. Another unfortunate reminder that old age had settled in. She took a moment to plan the rest of her day: she was going to get home, take a bath, call her son, and make dinner. A perfectly productive day. There was something else she knew she had to do, but for the life of her she couldn't remember.

She checked her rearview mirror and noticed something lying on the backseat. She turned around and confirmed that a can of corn was lying there. An escapee from the food drive. She sighed, too tired to run it back into the church. "Fine, we'll keep it." After finding her keys (they're in your hand, you old bat) she started her car and began the familiar drive back to the house.

The sitcoms these days didn't do much for Helen. She kept up with them regularly but rarely laughed at the jokes. She never remembered what had happened the week before, she was always barely paying attention. It was just a habit, a nightly ritual before she went to bed. The dirty plate from her dinner still sat on the kitchen table. She told herself she'd wash it in the morning, one of the perks of not having children or a husband around to give her flack for it. She was sitting back with her feet up on the ottoman, her trusty quilt covering her legs. The only light in the room came from the TV. Her kids told her that watching TV in the dark was bad for her eyes, but she figured she already wore glasses so what was the difference?

Sitting alone in the dark room Helen suddenly felt very alone. Even with the TV turned up and the sounds of the dryer running in the hall, the house felt quiet. Helen closed her eyes. She'd felt this way when her youngest child moved out: the empty nest syndrome. But back then she'd had Ronnie and together they'd found a new lease on life. Of course, then they were younger, and life was still exciting. Now that he was gone, Helen didn't know how to start a new chapter of her life. She was old now: this new chapter was the last chapter. What was she supposed to be doing in this part?

A sudden change in volume made her open her eyes. The forced laughter of the studio audience grew abruptly into the roar of a crowded stadium. Her sitcom had changed to a football game. She groaned a little to herself and started feeling around the couch for the remote. "Stop it, Ronnie!" she yelled at the TV. Finding the clicker and taking care to see which button she hit, she switched back to her regularly scheduled programming.

It was a commercial break, so she decided to go to the kitchen for a glass of water. After two attempts to stand up she shuffled over to the mantle that sat over a fireplace that had never been functional. She stopped there for a moment to look at the pictures. Her family when the kids were little, her adult kids with their families. She took an extra-long glance at her and Ronnie's wedding photo. So *young*. Such a handsome man, that mischievous smile. She was quite the looker, too. And look at how happy they were. The picture next to it was glossier and more recent: their 40th anniversary. Old people in that picture, but still happy and together.

Helen wiped the tears from her soft cheeks as she continued to the kitchen. She missed that man. Not a day went by she didn't think of him. But she knew they'd be together again soon enough. It's not like they were totally apart now anyway. When she returned to the living room the football game was back on. Shaking her head in defeat, she sat back down in the middle of the couch. She pulled the quilt up to her neck and leaned over to the right, where Ronnie used to sit. She sat like that and watched the football game, occasionally patting the cushion where Ronnie's leg should be. The loneliness softened a little.

The buzzing of the dryer didn't wake her up, and that was where she slept.

That Saturday saw a sudden heat hit the area. Summer was approaching, and that meant lawns would need upkeep. Last year was the first year she'd stopped asking her son to mow her yard and hired outside help. While she appreciated her son helping out, he was often too busy to keep up with it regularly. The hired help came in the form of Jim Walton, a boy of now eighteen. He was very polite, more than willing to mow her yard for a little extra cash. His mother had called earlier that week to see if Helen had wanted to hire him again for the summer. Helen happily agreed and said Saturday would be fine for the first mow of the year.

Jim was an attractive young man, dark brown hair and perfect teeth. In many ways he reminded her of Ronnie shortly after they'd started dating. Strong features and a friendly disposition. Ronnie had been so charming that she'd given him a second glance when she knew she shouldn't have. Jim was still quite young, life hadn't had a chance to wear him down yet.

They made polite small talk on the front porch. He gave her detailed answers about school and what his plans were after graduation. He was much more talkative than her own son had been at that age. When asked if he had a girlfriend he just laughed sheepishly, saying he didn't have time for things like that. Helen wondered if she'd embarrassed him by asking that, as if she were asking him for intimate details. She considered that maybe he had no interest in girls at all but didn't want to risk more embarrassment. Really, kids today think that old people are so out of touch.

She let Jim get to work on the mower in the shed out back. Told him to let her know if he had any trouble getting it started. Not that she could do anything herself, but she would let her son know so he could take a look at it later. She went back inside to clean up the kitchen. She promised herself she'd get it presentable before leaving to play Pinochle with Ruth and the girls. As she stood over the sink, she heard the mower roar to life. The sound got louder and closer as Jim began to take it in laps around the yard. She smiled with relief that she wouldn't have to bother her son about it.

She envied Jim for his abounding energy that he probably didn't appreciate. He was pushing a heavy machine around a yard on a hot day, while Helen was scrubbing her stove with an old sponge. The sad fact was they were both going to be tired when their tasks were done. What she would give for his stamina and his youth. To be able to jump and run and swim. And make love. The thought made her blush.

Right before she heard the yell she realized something was wrong. When did the mower shut off? How long had that noise been missing? She heard it now again, although something was different. Barely audible above the engine was the unmistakable sound of Jim screaming. Helen dropped her sponge on the stove and ran outside as fast as her bad knee would let her. She got to the yard to find the mower overturned, the blades still spinning. Next to it Jim was on his knees, clutching his hand against his chest. His white t-shirt was stained with that unmistakable dark red.

Helen's world became a blur. She started running towards Jim while fishing in her pocket for the cell phone her kids insisted she always have on her. She asked Jim what had happened, yelling to be heard over the engine and his screams. She didn't know why she asked; it didn't matter how it happened, what mattered was the result. Foolish questions asked in a panic.

Unable to get a response from the hysterical boy, Helen dialed 911 and told them to send an ambulance. She did her best to comfort him, but there was little she could do. Her limited experience in healthcare couldn't help her now; this was, as they say, above her paygrade.

When the paramedics came, one of them inspected Jim's hand while the other shut off the mower. Two of his fingers had been mangled horribly. Helen couldn't look, her stomach not as strong as it used to be. Through his sobs, Jim explained that the mower had stopped running so he flipped it over to see if it was clogged. He took the safety key out as a precaution, but somehow the thing had turned on while his hand was inside. The paramedics loaded him in the ambulance. Helen shouted after him that she would call his parents and let them know what had happened.

Mrs. Walton was panicked but kept enough sense to brush off Helen's tearful apology. "It's alright, Helen, it was an accident. Not your fault." She then hung up, running off to be with her son at the hospital. Helen poured herself a glass of red wine and sat down at the kitchen table. She was a little shaky, and surely her drinking so early in the day could be justified.

Had it been an accident? Helen didn't know if she believed in accidents like this. Anytime anything tragic happened the people at church always said, "It's all part of God's plan." They had told her that years ago, after her first miscarriage. They said it again when Ronnie died. It was a nice idea, that she was enduring these losses because God wanted to make her stronger or something.

Maybe she'd lost an unborn child so she would appreciate the kids she did have more. Maybe her husband of many years died so she could experience life while not being someone's wife. If this was all part of "God's plan," so be it. But poor Jim losing a finger in a lawn mower just seemed unnecessarily cruel. What good would it do to scar a nice young man like that? To cause him to possibly never play sports again, or even something as simple as playing a video game. If anything good were to come from it, Helen probably wouldn't live long enough to see it anyway.

The wine had calmed Helen down, her head felt a little heavier. Perhaps it wasn't God that hurt Jim. Maybe the Devil made it happen. Was it the Devil? Or someone else? She looked around the kitchen, as if expecting to see Ronnie standing somewhere looking guilty. "Did you hurt that boy, Ronnie?" she asked the empty room. There was no reply this time. Helen took the silence as an admission.

"That's a terrible thing to do." She said, brushing aside her guilt for admiring the young man's youth and body. Ronnie had always had a jealous streak, to put it mildly. It was one of the things she'd hated about him. The wine was hitting her a bit harder now. She decided to take a nap, and afterwards she would call up the Waltons and go see Jim at the hospital. Before she went to her bedroom, she called Ruth and told her she wouldn't make it to Pinochle today.

***

One had to wonder that if God's message was so important, why did it have to be given in such a boring way? Meggie Turner stifled another yawn behind her hand, being careful to make sure no one noticed. She tried to focus her gaze on Pastor Collins. Most people stared straight ahead during church and, if you didn't know better, you'd think they were actually listening.

Pastor Collins' words spoke of the kingdom of Heaven, but his voice was thin and weak. His teeth sat too far from each other, and he would whistle as he talked. When she'd first heard him preach, Meggie had to hold back the giggles. After a few Sundays she'd gotten used to it. It was almost soothing now, like falling asleep listening to the wind blow through your open window on a warm night. Except sleeping in church was frowned upon. That was the problem.

Sweat crept down her neck as the sermon kept chugging along. It was impossible to get back in after you've drifted off. Was he going on about the peace we'll find in Heaven or the tortures and brimstone of Hell? Same message every week, really: try to do right by other people so that you can ultimately go to a better place when you die.

In a sea of faces that were old and tired, Meggie's stood out. Most teens' Sunday best looked awkward on them, but Meggie thought she wore her dress well. She didn't look like a woman wearing little girl's clothes. The dress complimented her figure without showing it off. It was a bit too conservative to wear out with her friends, but she thought she looked good in it. Hottest girl in this church, that's for sure.

Meggie turned her head to look over at Ronnie. Ronnie Maye was the only other person her age that went to church. She was sure he found the sermon boring, probably wasn't even listening. Ronnie was there with his parents, same pew every week. His parents still sat on either side of him during services, as if he was a bad little boy who needed an eye kept on him. Meggie's parents were the only reason she was there, too. They came to church for appearances, and Meggie found it easier not to argue.

He slouched a bit, clearly not wanting to be there and not caring who knew. His clothes didn't suit him at all; his slacks were usually wrinkled, and his shirts bunched up at the bottom where he tucked them in. He could be mistaken for an overgrown child waiting to leave the pew.

Still, she had to admit, he was handsome.

They'd never spoken at church or at school. His family always left right after the services, she guessed Ronnie's father wanted to get home to his farm work. At school they rarely acknowledged each other. Maybe neither of them wanted to be the nerds that talked about church at school. She had friends and boys to be talking to, so a fleeting smile was all she ever gave to that sweet "church boy" Ronnie.

Ronnie noticed her looking at him. He looked a little startled to be getting attention from her. She gave him a wink, playful but not too suggestive. His face reddened as he smiled back. She turned back around, satisfied. It was too easy.

Meggie wasn't a regular face at the parties at the creek. She lived in town and driving out to the sticks to party never sounded appealing. Hanging out at the creek sounded like the kind of hick fun she dreamed to get away from. A few of her friends had gone, though, and reported back that they'd had such a fun time. The dark and dirty creek wasn't a terribly exciting atmosphere, but it was worth it for the lack of supervision. Her friend Hannah wanted to go up there this weekend, so Meggie agreed to accompany her.

The drive out was dreary, Meggie hated how dead the trees and hills looked at night. The site of the party was a bit more welcoming, lit up with a bonfire and the headlights of junky vehicles. She lit a cigarette for confidence as she got out of the car.

She grabbed two beers out of an ice chest and passed one to Hannah. The rest of the group welcomed them warmly. Hannah was blathering on, obviously nervous but trying to hide it. Meggie ignored her; she'll be fine. She started to scan the crowd for any familiar faces. A group of older boys had grouped up a ways away, smoking a joint. Jonny Delgado, who'd graduated last year, gave her a nod. She returned it but kept looking around. She'd go down that road as a last resort.

She knew Jonny a bit but never got to know him when they were at school together. He dressed like a "greaser," something not too common around here. She wasn't sure if he grew up somewhere else before relocating here, or if he was just trying to mimic the "cool" guys he saw in other cities. Wasn't something that Meggie was necessarily attracted to, but she supposed that the look suited Jonny. His confidence compensated for his lack of good looks.

A couple of farm boys had gathered around a truck near the fire. Meggie noticed Ronnie among them, and could see that he was staring at her again. She waved at him, and by the light of the fire could tell his face had reddened again. Smiling to herself, she walked over to join them.

"Hey Ronnie, how's it going?"

Ronnie looked surprised that she'd singled him out. Behind him his friends were sniggering to themselves. He gave her a friendly hello in return. His voice was deeper than she'd imagined it, more masculine. "It's nice to see you outside that damn stuffy church," Meggie continued, "those frumpy dress shirts don't do you justice." She put enough suggestion in her voice to make her point, sold it by reaching out and giving his forearm a pinch. She wasn't just putting him on though; he had quite the muscular form. All that farm work. Ronnie laughed a little too hard at her compliment.

They started talking freely about going to church, as no one else was listening to them anyway. Ronnie did a spot-on imitation of Pastor Collins, lisping through a passionate sermon about the evils of fornicating. He bummed a smoke off her, in what was probably an attempt to look cool. She guessed he'd never smoked before, going by the look on his face after that first inhale. Still a boy, not really a man yet. A lot of boys never became men. Maybe this one had a chance.

An hour or so later Ronnie and Meggie pulled into an empty field. She had suggested they leave together as the rest of the bonfire started to break up. He told her he knew a place and drove them to a secluded space, swerving slightly in his tipsiness. She left her car behind at the creek, and Hannah huffily got a ride home with someone else. She'd be fine.

It was a beautiful spot, she had to admit. It was surrounded by trees, but the clearing was wide enough that you could see the most stars. There were hundreds of them dancing against the dark sky. The moon was full and felt like it was closer to the earth than it'd ever been.

Ronnie dug out an old blanket that he kept behind the seats and they moved to the bed of the truck. They leaned against the back of the cab and she pressed against him under the blanket. They stared up at the stars, hopelessly trying to count them all. Occasionally one of them would say something, and the other would hum in agreement. Mostly they sat in silence.

Meggie made the first move when she realized the boy was too nervous to do it himself. She put her mouth over his and gently moved her tongue in. She rubbed the inside of his thigh while they kissed, took his hand and guided it to cup her breast. She thought he was going to explode right there, far too soon for her liking. When it seemed like he had finally adjusted she led him down that road.

The sex was awkward, like it often is the first time. He didn't know where to touch her, what parts to kiss and what not to. She took control, encouraged him when he needed it, directed him where to go and for how long. She played it up to boost his confidence; shuddered at his touch, moaned when he used his tongue. He almost yelled the first time she took him in her mouth. She continued at a comfortable pace, letting him adjust to the new sensation. Eventually he found his breath, relaxed but with curled toes.

She crawled on top of him, lit from above by the moonlight. They both gasped as he entered her; Meggie didn't know if she was acting anymore. They found their groove; he was focusing on her completely and it made things better for both of them. The truck was rocking with their movements, the only noise for miles around was their lovemaking. She reached her climax and thought maybe this town wasn't so bad after all. At least for this night.

He held her in his arms when they were done, naked under the blanket, looking at the stars once again.

Somewhere in the back of her mind she heard him say, "You're an angel Meggie."

Meggie had been the first girl in her class to kiss a boy, or so went the rumor. A week or so after the rumor she'd been given a reputation as a tramp. There'd been a falling out with her old group of friends. She made new friends after a while, Hannah and a few other silly girls. They didn't judge her, but they didn't understand her either. They were going to be content to start families right after school, didn't give much thought to things larger than themselves. But they were fun enough to hang out with for an afternoon.

Meggie was sure of three things: how many boys she'd actually kissed, how many she'd actually slept with, and how badly she wanted to leave this town.

Ronnie was a nice boy, and they'd spent a few good nights together. Turns out he was good company even when they weren't fucking. Decent sense of humor, a sweet disposition, all the things that make up a good person. But she could tell by his face he didn't know what she meant when she talked about leaving town. "Go where?" and "To do what?" he'd ask.

She'd walk around town sometimes when she was bored. She hoped that seeing other houses and people would lift her spirits, a change of scenery. Usually it ended up making her resentment worse. The houses weren't nice, they were just *there*. Some of them were totally rundown, boards in the windows and paint peeled off. Others were just suffering from the early signs of neglect. If all these houses were new and shiny, this town may actually look like a nice place to live. Was it a lack of money or a lack of time or a lack of interest?

The people on the street were friendly, kind of. They'd say "hello" as she passed them, or at least give a wave of recognition. Something about their energy put Meggie off. They looked tired all the time, as if they'd never known joy and convinced themselves they never would. Like maybe they wanted to leave too but didn't know how.

On this walk she spotted Jonny Delgado hanging outside the corner store. His dumb leather jacket looked a little small on him, his torn-up jeans looked more shabby than stylish. Definitely not as sexy as he thought he was. He approached her with a smile, letting his eyes pour over her body. She expected that; she was wearing the shorts her mother hated, after all. He offered her a smoke and she stopped to partake.

"I heard you were going 'round with that Ronnie kid," he asked. How subtle. A man two years out of high school still involved with the dating gossip. That's not very sexy.

"Yeah, kind of." The truth was Ronnie wanted to be her

boyfriend but didn't have the guts to up and ask her. That was fine with Meggie.

"So it's not serious?"

"No." She puffed her smoke, then decided to speak freely. "He'll never leave this town after high school."

"Oh, and you will?" He smiled, breathed the smoke out through his nose. A cute smile, but still not a handsome face.

"Absolutely."

Jonny stared at her, studying her, trying to see if she was serious. She smirked at him. They smoked. He broke the silence. "I think I'd like to leave someday too." He watched her face, eager to get her reaction to that. She kept her cool, though. He was posturing. Maybe he wanted to leave, but most likely this was a step on the journey to get into her pants.

"Really?" she asked. "You graduated a while ago; you're still here. What's kept you?"

He shrugged. "I don't know. Guess I'm just waiting on the right reason to go." Meggie resisted rolling her eyes. He was looking for sex. If she said she wanted to jump on a ship to Africa he'd agree to go with her. Maybe she could work with this.

She stomped out her cigarette on the sidewalk. "So, what are you doing this evening?" He grinned.

Jonny drove her home late that night. Would her parents be mad, or would they even notice? Didn't really matter. She could ask him right now to keep driving, get out of town with just his old car and the clothes on their backs. But they would probably need money eventually. No, better do some more planning.

She could convince him to leave town. He was the kind of guy who would do whatever a woman told him to. Not a feature she found attractive, but it would be helpful to her cause. Once they made it out, life would go from there. If they separated, so be it.

The sex had been different. Jonny had more experience than Ronnie but wasn't as tender with her. He had confidence in himself, that was for sure. His body had thick hair on his chest and stomach, while Ronnie was mostly hairless; the man and the boy. Ronnie had more muscles from the farm work, though; Jonny was softer. If she could only combine them into one person. He'd be a good-looking man with half a brain.

The streets were empty at this late hour. Good, didn't want to be seen with him. Not that she was embarrassed, just everyone knew she was going around with Ronnie. Two men is one too many, they'd call her a whore. If they didn't already. But then why should she care what they say anyway? She'd be out soon enough.

He kissed her goodnight. His mouth reeked of cigarettes, but then hers probably did too. She wondered if that's what Ronnie thought when he kissed her. A pang of guilt thinking about Ronnie. But they weren't dating, not really. This was still a betrayal though; he'd see it that way for sure. Boys get jealous.

She kept her eyes down as she walked from his car to her

house. The lights were off; her parents had gone to bed.

She couldn't see the stars through the roof of Jonny's car. It made the spot not as romantic as when Ronnie took her there. Jonny had wanted them to go somewhere outdoors, perhaps he was embarrassed by his dirty room (he should have been). Meggie thought maybe Jonny was trying to recapture the feeling of his high school days. She couldn't imagine wanting to relive high school, but she agreed and led them into the woods.

Maybe she should have felt more guilty about it, taking another boy to the spot Ronnie took her to. She had to admit it was tacky, but it really *was* a beautiful spot. And since Ronnie wasn't two-timing her like she was two-timing him, he wasn't likely to show up. The stars weren't as pretty tonight, though. More clouds than she would have liked.

She looked out through the window over Jonny's shoulder as he thrusted above her. Truth be told she'd gotten bored of the sex with him, but still felt she needed him. Over her few weeks with Ronnie, she'd managed to turn him into a great lover, or at least one that suited her needs. Jonny on the other hand… well, she tried to put the thought out of her mind while her head bumped lightly against the door handle.

Suddenly she felt the door open behind her, and a rush of the cool night air came into the car. She looked up and saw Jonny's surprised face a second before a fist knocked it back. Her screams were drowned out by Jonny's yelling and the grunting noises Ronnie was making as he threw more fists. She tried separating the two of them, but her position in the seat made it too awkward. She heard the opposite side door opening and felt Jonny jump out. Ronnie looked down at her, panting heavily. He had tears in his eyes.

"Whore."

He turned and left her with her tears. She grabbed her shirt and skirt off the floor and hastily pulled them on as she followed him out of the car.

Ronnie was in Jonny's face, swearing and screaming threats. Jonny had regained some composure and was starting to push back. His nose was bleeding, his face red with anger and the vulnerability of his nudity. He was being the tough guy, trying to intimidate Ronnie in spite of his bloody nose and softening penis. He was taunting Ronnie, insulting his manhood, implying he was incapable of satisfying Meggie like he was. He didn't notice the emptiness in the farm boy's eyes, but Meggie did. Ronnie was unrecognizable to her, like a man possessed. Meggie yelled at them to stop but neither could hear her. Ronnie charged and tackled the greaser, and they both went down. They tussled on the ground, throwing fists and clutching at throats.

Meggie could only watch from a distance, too afraid to get any closer. The stronger Ronnie had Jonny pinned down. She could see Jonny's arms swinging wildly, but only Ronnie's punches seemed to be landing. For all of Jonny's tough guy image, he was no match for the raw strength and fury inside of Ronnie. One of his hands swung out and backhanded Ronnie. It made him grunt but didn't slow him down in the slightest. If anything, it only intensified his anger.

She watched as both of Ronnie's hands shot down. His arms locked. Did he have a grip on Jonny's neck? Meggie couldn't tell from where she stood and could not make herself move closer. Ronnie lifted up his arms and then slammed them back down to the ground. A sickening noise rang out, a loud bang with a crunch. Jonny was screaming. Ronnie picked up the other man's head and slammed it down again. And again. And again.

The world was quiet now. Meggie had stopped screaming. Ronnie had stopped screaming. Jonny would never scream again. Even the crickets had stopped singing.

Ronnie turned to look up at her from where he still knelt on the ground. Tears were streaming down his face, and there was fresh blood too. It couldn't all be his. The rage had gone out of his eyes, and now there was nothing but fear. The little boy who'd lost his temper and now regretted what he'd done. He was pleading with her without saying anything. For a moment she felt bad for him, the poor stupid heartbroken kid. Then her instincts kicked in.

He kept staring at her as she ran to the front of Jonny's car and got in. She could see him, still kneeling over the body, in the rearview mirror as she drove off. She managed not to throw up until she got home. Her parents, for once concerned about where she'd been all night, demanded to know what happened. She told them everything through fresh tears. Her mother held her close to her and kept holding her close as she retold the story to the police.

***

The sun was coming in strong today through the little window in Ronnie's room. It was going to be a beautiful day. Hopefully he'd get to go outside and enjoy it. He shifted in his little bed, trying to get comfortable. He couldn't get rid of the knot in his back.

A knock at the door, a courtesy because they always come in anyway. It was that new nurse, carrying a breakfast tray.

"Good morning, Ronnie." She had a nice little voice. A ray of sunshine in such a gloomy place. Obviously new to the profession, not cynical like the older nurses. "Here's your eggs and your pills."

"Is it nice outside today?" he asked her. He took the little cup of pills and downed them, chasing them with a splash of orange juice. She watched him to make sure they all went down. Others hated taking their pills, but not Ronnie. Pills kept the anger away, kept the bad down. He remembered what he did; he knew he was lucky to be here and not somewhere worse.

The nurse smiled. "It's beautiful today, Ronnie." She took the cup back and left the food plate. Ronnie watched her as she went to leave.

"What was your name again?"

She turned and looked back at him politely. "Helen.

Remember?"

"Of course, Helen. Thank you, Helen."

She left. Ronnie laid back down, ignoring his breakfast. He stared at the little window, imagining what life would be like when he was free. He would find atonement in the eyes of the law but wasn't sure if he'd find it in himself. That night had stayed with him all this time. A lot of people would always see him as a monster; the girl's family had made sure of that. But he believed he could move forward, still have a decent life. Even if he didn't deserve one.

He'd never be able to fully escape his past. He saw the greasy boy's face in his dreams most nights. Then the bloody remains of his face, and the screaming of the girl. Felt like something out of a movie, but he knew it had actually happened. He'd been told it happened, and may God forgive him. He spent most of his days here asking for forgiveness.

The girl…Meggie. They always told him to use her name when he talked about her, to remind him that she is a real person. She always spoke about moving somewhere else, wanting to start a whole new life. He hadn't understood her back then. Now, ironically, he knew exactly how she felt.

He thought about the life he wanted to live. A "normal" life, in a town far from where he grew up. Where he could start fresh, where no one knew him. He'd be better, he'd keep taking his pills. It wouldn't happen again. He'd find a job, maybe a nice woman. Maybe he'd marry, have some kids.

He'd been gifted a second chance, due to his youthfulness and some insanity plea or some other legal phrase he hadn't fully understood. He could never fix what he did to the families involved, would never get forgiveness from Meggie. But he had recently vowed, to himself and to God, he would spend every day of the rest of his life to try and be the best person he could be. It's all he could do. It's all anyone can do.

Ronnie looked back out of his window at what little of the world he could see. It was going to be a nice day.

Ev'ry Summer in July

Gather 'round, folks, and give me your ear. I'll tell you the story 'bout how music came to these here hills.

It was many years ago on a hot July day. The townspeople were sweating and bored, hiding in their homes to escape the scorch of the sun. It'd been like that all summer. It was so hot nobody wanted to wander outside for anything. The air was thick like gravy and the grass was more brown than green. People reluctantly went to work in the morning as the sun just started to creep up. By the evening, everyone was too exhausted to go anywhere or socialize. They were worn out, they were irritable, and they had no damn idea what to do with themselves.

But then one day a stranger came to town. No one knew where he came from or what business he had there. He was a young fella, sorta on the skinny side. He wore a wide-brimmed straw hat that covered his eyes, the tip of which almost touched the bridge of his thick nose. A pair of overalls with no shirt underneath, so the world could see his dark and lanky arms. His feet were bare and, judging from the scars and dried blood on them, he'd probably never owned a pair of shoes. He held an old moonshine jug down by his side, gripping the neck with long, dirty fingers.

The man started strolling around town and lookin' at the houses. There were no people on the streets, no kids playing out in the yards. Some folks peeked out at him from behind their windows. Most of them were scared, thought he was a strange drunk mountain man that had wandered into town to cause trouble. Strangers weren't common in this neck of the woods. Outsiders didn't have much of a need to come to them. The townsfolk kept to themselves and liked it that way.

The man's hazel eyes scanned the houses. It was like he could sense the unhappiness in the air. He could see them through the walls and the glass of their homes. He looked through the heat and exhaustion and saw deep inside them. Into their tired, beaten-down souls. There was something else eatin' away at the townsfolk. They were lacking something. They had a longing.

He kept walking through the streets. No one spoke to him or bothered him, just watched him stroll in confused silence. Eventually he circled back to the edge of town towards the hills. He turned back around to face the town, the mountains behind him lit up by the orange sunset. The heat was dropping finally, just beginning to be tolerable.

The man shot out his bright pink tongue quickly, like a snake tasting the air. Satisfied, he slowly wet his full, chapped lips. He brought the jug up to his mouth. He took a deep breath, pursed his lips, and blew over the top of it.

A low, hollow tone rang out. It wasn't the prettiest sound, but it was strong. It echoed through the streets. It reached the people sitting in their homes and made them look up in confusion. The noise went through their ears and into their chests, reverberating somewhere in their stomachs. It broke their concentration; it made their hands shake in excitement. It was a sound the townspeople hadn't heard in a long time.

It was music.

He blew the jug again. And again. A few people thought it was a train, before remembering there weren't any tracks for at least a hundred miles. As if waking up from a long slumber, the people left their homes. They were looking up and around, trying to find the source of this new sound. While they were searching, they made eye contact with their neighbors. They smiled, they shook hands, they said things like, "What do you 'spose that is?" They formed little groups with their friends. Those little groups joined up with other little groups. Eventually a large crowd had gathered and started walking towards the edge of town, towards the mysterious young stranger with his jug.

The corners of his mouth turned up into a smile as he kept blowing on the jug. Without a word, he turned around and started walking out of town. The townspeople followed on foot, confused and giddy. They were all together, so nobody was afraid of following a stranger into the hills at night.

They walked on through the hills, passing by the houses of the farmers and other folks who lived on the outskirts of town. The man kept blowing his jug, spreading that simple music around. The hill folk, after some initial shock, joined in with the townspeople. The crowd was getting bigger and bigger. A wild energy was passed between them, their suffering from the sun now forgotten. For the first time all summer, the people were excited.

They kept walking for an hour or so. Nobody thought to yell ahead and ask the man where they were going. They didn't want to interrupt his jug-blowing, didn't want that sound to go away. A few of them got a little nervous, wondering just how long they were going to walk through the hills. Still, none of them would turn around and go back; they had to see this through to the end.

Finally, the stranger stopped the mob at a large clearing. He turned around and faced the crowd he'd summoned. He removed the jug from his lips and lazily returned it to his side. The crowd kept looking at him, a sea of expectant and bemused smiles. They kept silent, waiting and watching the man to see what he'd do next. You could almost taste their anticipation.

The stranger looked up, his eyes glowing bright in the last of the setting sunlight. He glared at the crowd before him, scanning them for something in particular. His eyes finally rested on Stevie, a quiet teenager not many people knew that well. Stevie's eyes met the stranger's. The man nodded an invitation.

Stevie approached the front of the crowd, clutching a fiddle in his sweaty hand. Stevie had been practicing alone at home when the townspeople were gathering, and in his excitement to join them he'd held onto his instrument. Seeing the encouraging faces of the stranger and the crowd, Stevie lifted the fiddle to his chin and began to play.

Nobody had ever heard Stevie play the fiddle before, except for his family. It was something he kept to himself for fear of being made fun of at school. He loved playing fiddle most in the world but was too embarrassed to tell people that. He never thought about performing in public, let alone in front of the whole town, but the crowd's eagerness gave him the confidence to play like he'd never played before.

His fiddle sang out into the night sky, notes leaping around the open valley and dancing off into the mountains. The fiddle, much more so than the simple jug, affected the townspeople. They started to clap along; some even began to dance. Soon they were all hooting and hollering and having a good ol' time. There was the occasional sharp note or wrong string, but no one minded. It didn't matter that Stevie wasn't a perfect musician. Most had forgotten what music sounded like, and to them it was the most beautiful sound in the world.

Emboldened at what was happening, other musically inclined folk were inspired to go fetch their instruments and join Stevie. Some of them ran all the way back to town, returning to the clearing in record time. The first one to make it back was a man with a banjo, who quickly joined in with the fiddle to create an upbeat jig. Soon after a woman with an upright bass joined them, keeping the rhythm in line and fleshing out the sound. Before long a full band had formed: people had guitars, banjos, fiddles, spoons…it had become a regular ol' hootenanny. When musicians got tired, other people would jump in to replace them.

There were no moments of silence or stillness. A steady stream of music flowed through the mountains. A number of talented musicians strummed, picked, and plucked their hearts out. Percussion was supplied by someone scratching on a washboard or clacking spoons against their hands. Most people thought the spoons were stupid, but they were in such a good mood nobody really cared. Although, the two-minute spoons solo did seem to go on a little long.

Some of the townspeople who weren't musicians – the "audience", you could call 'em, realized that the moon and stars weren't going to provide enough light. Materials were gathered and soon a series of bonfires scattered the clearing, giving visibility to the musicians and warmth from the now-chilly night air. It was hard to believe mere hours ago everyone had been so hot they could hardly stand it. Now here they were, dancing and working up a sweat around a campfire.

Then the singing started. A man started yodeling along with the band, to the delight of the crowd. A line quickly formed as singers felt emboldened to come forward and show off their skills. They wanted to sing the old folk songs their parents taught them that had been passed down for years. Others wanted to sing their favorite hymn, or their favorite popular song. If the current batch of musicians didn't know the tune, they would sub out for someone who did. While the next singer was deciding what song to sing, the guitars and banjos would have a quick picking session.

But it wasn't just a party. Some of the performers went up and bared their souls. The people in town that tended to get forgotten about: folks who'd lost a spouse, lost a child, had parents who'd lost their minds. The lives that had been particularly painful lately, and they let their pain out in song. It moved many in the crowd to tears.

Everyone danced wildly for hours, until finally things started to wind down against the hypnotic voice of a singing saw. New singers and musicians were discovered that night. The townspeople had danced together, laughed together, cried together. For the first time in a long time they felt like a community, instead of just people who happened to live in the same area. The world can be a wonderful place, even when it gives you pain. We're all in this together, folks, and that night those people felt that.

No one noticed that the strange man who'd brought them all together had vanished into the night. Few would later claim that they could make out his silhouette watching them from high up in the mountains. Some made elaborate guesses about where he'd come from. Maybe he was an angel sent to bring music to them, or simply just a kind, wise fellow with a jug. No one ever laid eyes on him again, but those in the clearing that night would always thank the stranger who'd assembled their little jamboree.

The following year the townspeople returned to the clearing to hold another concert in July. Spurred on by the memories of the last time, people invited friends and family to come join in on the festivities. The turnout was much higher than it had been the first year. It was just as good as they remembered, with a few encore performances from last time plus plenty of new folks jumping in. Over the course of the last year, many people had learned how fun music could be and had taken up instruments of their own. At the end of that night everyone went back to their houses, exhausted but just as satisfied as they'd been the year before.

This tradition repeated summer after summer. Soon people from nearby towns heard about it and would travel over to satisfy their curiosity. Everyone would have a fun time and go back home and tell their friends and neighbors about it. Word got out, and soon people from out of state started making the trip up every summer. The party was growing; the music continued to touch everyone in attendance each and every year.

However, some of the folks who'd gone to the original gathering would moan about how it just wasn't the same anymore. While more people should mean more fun, the "original" fans felt like they were being trespassed upon. All these people coming into their town just to take part in their concert seemed rude. If they wanted good music, why didn't they just make their own?

"Nonsense!" others would say. "This is a beautiful thing we've got going here, why shouldn't we share it with everybody?" That was the general consensus, so the grumblings of a few townsfolk were ignored in favor of keeping everyone happy. The more the merrier, after all.

The crowds kept coming. They brought with them more traffic and a mess to clean up afterwards. They clogged up the roads, didn't pick their trash up when they left. The vegetation in the clearing started to suffer; the audience area became a giant mud pit thanks to the constant foot traffic. After a few years, a lot of the locals stopped going to the show, unable to tolerate the mess and the hassle.

As the party kept growing, so did the conflicts. The bands and singers started to argue about performance times. Too many musicians wanted the "good spots" when they would get the crowd at its liveliest. Someone had the idea to start making up a schedule, but it was difficult to make one that pleased everybody. Soon they realized there were too many acts to fit into one night, so the event expanded from one night to two, then later still to three. What had started as one night to let loose and have fun was now becoming an elaborate weekend festival.

Now as harsh as it is to say, not all the musicians were the same caliber. Some were too inexperienced, hadn't found their voices yet. Letting them play for a half hour was too demanding of them and not enjoyable for the crowd. Audiences started to get bored with acts they didn't think deserved to be there. So, to make the underwhelming acts more enjoyable, people started bringing their own refreshments: moonshine, whiskey, beer. Usually by midnight every song would get thunderous applause, as the crowd was too drunk to be able to tell the good from the bad.

Like all big events and occasions, someone eventually had to take charge. There came about a bidding war for property rights to the clearing. It was eventually bought out by the son of one of the men who'd attended the original gathering, who'd been raised on his father's stories about what a fun and momentous occasion that night had been. Hoping to bring that experience to further generations, the son had a proper stage built in the clearing for the bands to perform on. Though the big festival would still only take place in the summer, other events and concerts could be rented out on the stage year-round.

Soon the descendants of one of the town's most favorite men were charging admission. They needed money, they claimed, to bring out-of-town acts in to "headline" the concerts. At first this excited the local musicians: the chance to perform alongside professionals! A few of them benefited from that; they made connections, moved out to Nashville or wherever, and went on to have big music careers of their own. The spectators were just as excited at the idea of all these world-famous musicians coming to perform in their little neck of the woods. The town was now reaching attention on a national level, at least to fans of good ol' fashioned hillbilly music.

The festival grew to such a level that professional musicians all over the country wanted a piece of the action, not to mention the money. More and more bigger names were accepted in the interest of creating a larger draw. Locals were no longer allowed to just bring their fiddle and play. You had to go through agents, managers, people who had rates. Someone in charge had to decide if your talent was good enough to deserve any of that coveted stage time. Ticket prices went up as the shows got "bigger and better," until people had to start saving up their cash year-round to afford it.

Something happens to people when they start spending money: they get the idea that because they spent so much, they're entitled to do whatever they want. And at the festival, that was pretty much true. People would bring three days' worth of alcohol and drink it all on the first day. They'd be rowdy and rambunctious for hours, until they'd finally pass out. After sleeping it off and before the next night's festivities began, they'd run out and procure more alcohol to repeat the process all over again. They were a rowdy group now, but it was all in good fun. Who didn't occasionally toss their cookies at a concert, right?

Decades after it started, the festival had taken on a life of its own. It wasn't just a festival anymore: it was an *event*. It was a *holiday*. People planned their summers around it. They would take their vacations during that week, they would call off work, they would have countdowns as soon as the new year started. It was broadcast on all the news and radio stations. A camping site was added near the stage. The regulars took trailers there and camped all weekend, three consecutive days of nonstop music and drinking.

Conversations about the festival began to change. Nobody mentioned the acts they listened to or the stories that touched them. Now the stories were all the worst kinds of stories: Drinking stories. Stories that start with "Oh man, we had so much *beeeeeer.*" Stories that revolved around finding a funny place to throw up, like in your friend's shoes or some girl's hair. Dramatic retellings of the origins of a few bruises and a bloody nose. How you and your friends heroically beat up someone else who was giving you a hard time. Some young ladies had stories about the men that would "flirt" with them for all three days. In the luckier stories, the men eventually stopped.

There were silly drinking games, mostly centered around people potentially hurting themselves on obstacle courses or mud pits. When you're drinking you don't always remember to do things like apply sunscreen, so by the end of the weekend you've got a fresh new sunburn and increased odds of getting skin cancer. The long-term fans are easily recognized by their brown, leather-like skin that they happily show off in revealing clothing. If you could say one nice thing about the crowd that forms at the concert in the last few decades, they are all very confident and comfortable with their bodies. An unofficial dress code developed for the festival: short shorts, wife-beaters, t-shirts sliced from the shoulder to the hip, jeans with holes in them, cargo shorts, and other things of that nature. Things designed to keep you cool but you also wouldn't mind if it got mud or vomit on it. And it's all topped off with cowboy hats and boots.

Although, truth be told, the average concert goer had little in common with the cowboys of old.

Even though it had changed a lot since that first hot night, one thing stayed the same: the jamboree brought people together. Relatives would go together as an annual tradition. Many happy marriages started their relationship at the concerts, and surely a few lives were conceived there. Most people in the surrounding area can look back at the happy times they had listening to music among the mountains. It was a rite of passage: like hunting, but louder.

As the world kept turning and lives kept changing, so did the music. Music is an always-evolving creature, one of the greatest wonders of the world that often gets taken for granted. Because, folks, music comes from within a person. That person has an idea, a thought, a message, a story they want to tell. They write notes for it, add accompaniment, make it so their audience can feel what they're feeling. If it's a happy feeling, they spread joy. If it's a sad feeling, they comfort others by reminding them they're not alone. Music incites emotions in others. It is powerful enough to heal the soul.

But the acts at the festival had changed over the years too. People liked to party and have a good time, and most of them only ever wanted to hear songs about partying and having a good time. The so-called "professional" musicians are often pressured to write such music to appeal to that demographic. They sing of the "simple life" and other vague relatable issues to trick listeners into thinking they're one of them. What ends up happening is a lot of those concerts end up sounding what we call "commercial." Close your eyes and you can't tell one from the other: the voices sound the same, the songs sound the same, the lyrics are about the same things. Often a song will stand out when it promotes aggressive patriotism or bolsters masculinity, and that song can stay on the airwaves for years after it comes out. The result is that more unique individuals have a hard time getting noticed. Their voices get drowned out among the Kennys, Garths, and Lukes. Music has the potential to heal the soul, but the business of music can crush one. And that is how a lot of old-timers feel about that festival nowadays: No soul.

Now I didn't mean to preach there; I just miss the music sometimes. It's gotten harder to find, you see.

After years of having to clean up the cigarette butts, the red solo cups, the beer bottles, someone finally said, "Enough is enough." It wasn't about the music anymore, people just wanted to get drunk and make a mess. As any child will tell you, parents eventually get tired of cleaning up after you. Tired and annoyed citizens made petitions and brought them to the fellas in charge. They suggested decreasing the amount of people that could come, putting limits on the amount of alcohol they could consume, and heavily encouraged putting local and unknown acts onto the stage. They had grown up listening to stories about the original concert, and they were trying to capture that magic of the night they'd heard about.

The producers outright ignored the request to reduce capacity; that was how they made their money, after all. They agreed to ban alcoholic refreshments from the stage area and cancel the BYOB policy that had put them on the map. This was obviously a way for them to make more money on their own alcohol sales and not in the interest of helping others. They said they'd "think about" putting newer artists on the stage.

The alcohol restrictions were met with an outcry of disdain and hate. What was this, prohibition all over again? There were rights and traditions that this festival had been founded on! The fans had strength in numbers, so the folks in charge relented and reversed their decision. In the end, nothing had changed. Oh, how the happy drinkers were so pleased with themselves for making their voices heard as one.

Their efforts were in vain, however. The following year all the bigwigs in charge went into negotiations about renewing the property lease. Few know what went on in those talks, but ultimately an agreement was never reached. The event has not been held since. Fans all over the state and country were crushed by the decision. It was like canceling the Super Bowl.

The folks in town haven't minded its absence, really. They try to make more efforts to socialize with their friends and neighbors, but in smaller ways. A book club, a poker game, the usual things. Nothing that could explode into a week-long tourist destination.

I sometimes go to the hillside where it used to be. I've heard rumors that once in a while you can spot the dark skinny barefoot man who led the original townspeople there, strolling around the deserted field. Obviously, that's a bunch of bull, he would be long dead by now. But a little part of me hopes that somehow, it's true. Maybe he can teach the current residents that they don't need to pay money and drink to feel alive. They have something inside of them and they don't even know it.

So, folks, that's the story of how music came to these here hills. And also how it came to leave. I hope one day I'll be able to tell you the story of how it came back.

Void

"I NEED A VOID UP FRONT, PLEASE."

I cringe a little as I hear my voice reverberating throughout the store. No one likes hearing the sound of their voice on a recording, but just as bad is hearing it over a PA system. I sound weak and the speakers amplify my neediness for the whole world to hear. My assistant manager, Patty, has a better voice for announcements; it's unnaturally high and sweet-sounding, adds a bit of sugar to whatever she says. It's served her well during her long tenure in customer service.

I stare at my ugly customer, who is annoyed that I had to pause our transaction to page somebody. As a low-level "associate" I have to page a manager for almost everything. If someone is returning an item, if I make a mistake on the register, if I need a void. This time it wasn't my fault; for whatever reason this idiot decided she didn't want a bag of chips after I'd already scanned it.

The time between my page and a manager showing up feels like an eternity. When Rodney finally gets there, he punches in that coveted four-digit code and the void is done. All that paging and waiting just for a fix that's over in four seconds. I finish the transaction and the customer leaves, still annoyed at the inconvenience. I mumble "Have a nice day" at her back. As if I care. Is there a bigger lie in the world than when a cashier says,

"Have a nice day"?

Rodney grumbles something in my direction as he walks back to what he'd been doing. I assume it was nothing about me personally. Rodney is a nice enough older man, but a bit of a grump. He's worked for the company a long time and has a few gripes with some of their policies. While we all can get annoyed with his grumpiness, I think we appreciate his lack of enthusiasm for the dumber rules. For example, a "company meeting" involves him coming up to you and saying something like, "Hey we're supposed to double bag these things now. That was a meeting, if anyone asks." We're not one of those enthusiastic teams that would be featured in an employee training video.

After he's left me alone, I go back to looking busy behind the counter. My line is empty now; it's a slow day. The majority of the stocking was done earlier in the morning, so I'm left to busy myself with whatever little cleaning tasks I can find. I usually get most of them done in an hour and then get bored for the rest of my shift. Not that it matters when Rodney's here, he usually spends his time in the office looking busy. I have my book tucked away under the register to sneak a few pages later. A few pages of a book are a small distraction, but it's enough to help me get through it.

I look at the clock and try to figure out how many hours I have before I leave. Oh fuck. It's Friday. I'm doubling today. I forgot. The days have bled together this week. But I remember now; a double shift Friday followed by a morning shift Saturday.

What a fun weekend.

Every time you enter the store all color vanishes from the world. Took me a whole year to figure that out. Sure, you think you see colors: the bright yellow of the sales tags, the gray-tan of the metal shelves, the aisle full of gaudy holiday decorations. But look closer, under the endless rows of long fluorescent lights, the whole store seems like it's inside a faded TV screen. It's like when Dorothy leaves the vibrant colors of Oz and finds herself back on the boring, devoid-of-Technicolor farm.

I stare outside the big windows at the sun setting on the parking lot. For once, there are no stray buggies sitting out there for me to go and collect. I look at my shitty car, Rodney's shitty car, some anonymous shitty cars, and a nicer car that belongs to the pharmacist. I look down at the corner of the window and contemplate dusting the ledge today. They always need dusting.

I decide to pull out the handheld Swiffer and pretend to dust for a while. I keep doing this, stopping to ring up a few straggling customers, until Rodney comes back to put me on my break. Lunch today is those little Easy Mac bowls that you add water to and microwave, because I forgot to pack a lunch and forgot I was working a double. I shamble off to the tiny break room in the back, the break room that was never supposed to exist. I think it was a bathroom when the place was originally built. It fits a small table with the microwave on it, two small chairs, and nothing else. The only real comfort it provides is solitude. I stir the powdered cheese into my hot cup of noodles and water, kicking myself again for not making a real lunch ahead of time.

As I slurp down my preservative-filled mac and cheese I wonder what Mom will make herself for dinner tonight. I just hope she makes a lot of it and keeps some on the stove for me. What's the point of going through the embarrassment of living with your mother if you can't get a nice dinner once in a while, right?

Living with Mom isn't as bad as it sounds. She gripes at me from time to time, but she treats me like an adult, mostly. I pay rent and contribute to the bills. It's like being roommates with someone who just happened to give birth to you. It's not the coolest, most ideal situation but I'm not the only one of my friends who still lives with their parents. And some of my friends have crazy-ass parents. I'm among the luckier ones, I think.

Mom never gets on my case about work. She's worked at a grocery store most of her life. As long as I'm bringing home a paycheck she doesn't care where it's from. If I'm not selling drugs or selling my body, then we're all good. The drugs are a fair concern, god knows this town has the demand for it and I do have access to pills. But to be a whore, in this town? I deserve better clientele.

On days like this I wonder why corporations decided that having cashiers sit down looks lazy. Why can't we sit down while working the register? You can get right back up afterwards. My foot pain is awful and I'm the youngest employee here. I try not to bitch about it because I imagine they're suffering worse. I think other countries let their cashiers sit down. Cashiers sit down at Aldi. I wish I'd gotten that job at Aldi. Everyone at an office job gets to sit down. Everyone likes a nice sit. Eight hours in a row is a long time on your feet, and a fifteen-minute sit in a metal folding chair doesn't do much to alleviate that. As long as I don't take too long, I've learned I can sit on the milk crates behind the registers and rest my sore feet if no one is around.

We aren't busy this afternoon, so it goes by slowly. Patty is doing her usual checklist of managerial duties in the back half of the store, so I'm free to stroll around the front half and look busy. I let my "OCD" take over and I fix the candy at the front counter that had been moved around and no longer lines up with the sales tags. It's a menial task but it looks so much better when I'm done. Not that it really matters; candy sells itself.

Patty comes back up to check on me and make small talk for a while. I enjoy Patty. She's worked here for a long time; she calls herself a "lifer." She likes to joke that one day, when she's ready, she'll just crawl into the corner of the store and die. I remember when I first started working here a year ago and she asked me what I wanted to do with my life. I'd sighed and shrugged a little as an answer. I told her I didn't know yet. I wasn't sure.

"Well you can't work here your whole life," she said in mock concern. "I have, and look at me." She widened her eyes at me to make herself look crazed. Then we laughed. A good sense of humor, that Patty. A more positive attitude than most customer service lifers; like she wakes up in the morning and just chooses to be happy.

I can't imagine being a lifer anywhere. Last summer I worked for a construction company, turning that STOP/SLOW sign all day. The money was alright and the work was easy, but I knew I couldn't do that my whole life. It was still upsetting when they laid me off along with some others. I had to start applying for whatever jobs I could find, whoever was hiring. A quick interview with Rodney and then here I was: a new part-time employee. Now it's been a year and I have a few more weekly hours but still not enough to qualify for full-time. And my pay is now thirty cents over minimum wage. Only took a year. I wonder how much I'd make if I were a lifer, and how long it would take to get there.

I take my dinner break in my car because I can't spend one more minute in that tiny break room. I get a quick meal (a pepperoni roll and a Diet Coke) from the gas station next door. After I finish scarfing down the roll, I light up a nice late-shift smoke. I'm a little tense. I'd had to deal with a rude fat woman who insisted that the Reese's Cups were, "Buy one, get one free." I explained that the sales tag on them was left over from *last* week, as it said on the tag.

"Well take the damn sign down!" she snarled at me before waddling out of the store. I don't know what her problem was;

clearly we'd just missed a tag from last week. It was an annoying mistake, but nothing worth swearing at a person over. I guess when you're fat and can't get four peanut butter cups for the price of two you get a little cranky.

As I flicked ash out of my window I noticed Carl the FedEx guy coming into the store. Carl is the closest thing to sex appeal I get to look at on a regular basis. He's in his late thirties, his skin tanned from driving around all day with the window down. He has a tattoo of something in Arabic on his neck. I've thought of asking him what it means but I don't want the answer to be something douchey like "courage" or lame like "respect." He keeps his sunglasses on inside, which usually is an asshole move but he counters it by always flashing a smile. His teeth aren't great but, compared to what I usually see, they are acceptable.

He always flirts with me when I sign for the packages. Well, I mean he smiles at me. I suffer from a social disease where I think anyone who smiles at me is flirting with me. Mom has told me, "No, honey, some people are just friendly people who smile at strangers." How odd.

Whenever I'm the one who signs for deliveries Carl repeats my name back to me, then shoots me with little finger guns and says, "Have a good one." My eyes follow him out, taking in his muscular calves covered by white socks that go up to his knees. I fantasize about his thighs and butt being equally muscular, but they remain a mystery thanks to those lumpy work shorts.

I get bummed that I'm missing his visit today because I'm

smoking in the car. I think about going in before my break is over, acting like I forgot something inside. I decide against it, preferring the comfort of the soft car seat to teasing my horniness with a few glances. After a few seconds Carl comes back out. As he crosses the lot he looks over and sees me in my car. He lifts his chin in recognition and gives a little wave.

I wave back. My stomach churns. I finish my smoke.

The evening half of a Friday usually gets busy. Becky and Patty jumped onto the other registers to help the long line go a little faster. It's hectic but we manage fine. Shifts usually go by faster when we're busy, but that also means you have to talk to more customers. Put on your smile, answer their questions, listen to their complaints. I'm not always in the mood to talk to these people, but it's like 80% of my job.

I see Ashley, the pharmacy assistant, leaving. I remember her from high school, even though we were never friends or anything. She gives me a polite smile and a wave goodnight as she exits. I return the wave, jealous that she gets to leave early because the pharmacy closes early. Sometimes I wish I worked in the pharmacy section instead of the front end. The hours are shorter, and I'm sure that the pay is better. But then I remember all the angry old people I see storming back towards the pharmacy and decide I'm better off. Plus, I don't know if I'm the kind of person who would steal pills, so I probably shouldn't put myself in a situation where I could find out.

One of my favorite semi-regulars comes in tonight. He's this younger guy, looks straight out of high school, if he's not still in it. He does the same thing every time he comes in: He nervously buys condoms. It takes him forever. He'll pace in front of the pharmacy shelf where the condoms are before finally grabbing a box and walking up to me at the register. Sometimes he'll grab a Twix bar or some deodorant to try and distract me from the black ribbed-for-her-pleasure rubbers. He always has a sort of sheepish look on his face, like he's getting away with something naughty.

Tonight he brings up more items than usual. There's the usual deodorant, a few snacks, the inconspicuous condoms. Oh, and what's this? Lube! He's learning. It's the cheap brand, though. I get that he's young and doesn't want to spend money, but this is a moment where you should treat yourself to a name brand. How do I tell him that? And why should I? Here he is, young with an active sex life, and here's me, getting older and less active by the day. I bag up his cheap lube. I hope it burns them.

The day is over. I take a minute to just sit in my car, let my feet rest, and smoke. I stare at the empty store in front of me. It looks so different with all the lights turned off.

When I finally get home I learn that I'm out of luck. No dinner in sight and Mom's bedroom door is shut. I can faintly hear the news on the TV in her room. I take a Hot Pocket from the freezer and heat it up. The first bite is mozzarella lava, the inside bites are cold. I hate these things, why do I keep buying them?

I watch TV in the living room and drink a beer. I text a few of my friends to see if anyone's free. Of course no one is. Half of them have kids and are busy with their kids, putting their kids to sleep, feeding their kids, blah blah blah kids. The ones that don't have kids are busy too, with their own degrading jobs and exhausting lives. I wasn't expecting anyone to actually hang out with me; I've already taken off my shoes and pants for the night.

The late-night lineup goes by quickly on TV. Jokes that aren't funny and celebrities I don't recognize. I'm only watching it so that I don't have to go to bed right away. If I go to bed right away, then it's like all I do is work and sleep. That's no life. When the syndicated sitcom reruns come on I know it's officially well past midnight. I can hear mom's snores through her door as I head to my room. I crawl into bed, the same bed I crawled into during high school, and close my eyes.

I oversleep the next morning. I pull on my ugly brown button-up and leave, saying a quick goodbye to Mom. She's sitting at the kitchen table with her coffee. She's looking tired today, I think. I get in my car and start speeding off to work, lighting my morning cigarette as I go. I catch my reflection in the rearview mirror. I look tired today too.

I park in the corner of the lot at work and dig my nametag out of the glove compartment. I get to the glass door of the store and start knocking, waiting for whoever is in charge this morning to let me in. Some days I knock on the door for a long time like a crazed Mormon missionary. By the time I'm contemplating having another smoke Patty shows up to let me in. She gives me a friendly "Hello!" which I try to return. Such a morning person, I don't know how she does it.

I have about ten minutes to get ready, which is mainly just tucking my book in a little space below the counter. I check to see if I have enough plastic bags to get me through the morning. There isn't a group of people standing outside waiting to come in, so we're already lucky today. A lot of townies like to get the jump on us, be first in line to grab their prescriptions or have a money order made.

I spend the first few hours of my morning dealing with the regular round of drunks doing some late prepping for the weekend. I realize yesterday must have been pay day for a lot of folks. Every customer is well over forty so I'm constantly typing in my own birthday when the computer asks me to check IDs. Quicker that way.

I see one of our regulars, a quiet and gruff man, come in for his usual order. He always gets a four-pack of the tallboy Heineken cans. Never any other quantity or any other brand, and I don't remember him ever getting anything else with his beer. I wonder if he's drinking in secret, maybe hiding something from a wife or kids. I wonder why he never stocks up. Maybe it's a routine for him. Just drink the four big cans and be done with it.

I try to guess who is having a party this weekend and who is gonna drink by themselves, who is a social drinker and who's a drunk. The ones that smell like stale alcohol and body odor are the most obvious. They're likely to buy their tall boys with mostly change. It takes them forever to count out their quarters, dimes, nickels, and fucking pennies. Sometimes I walk down to the other end of the counter and pretend to grab something while they count out their total, just to get away from the smell. I throw their coins in my drawer without checking it. I tell them, "Have a nice day," and then discreetly sanitize my hands.

Some of the drunks are a bit more subtle about it. Like Mrs. Wilcox, an old woman who either became crazy from drinking or was crazy before she turned to drinking. She shuffles in on a weekly or bi-weekly basis. She waves hello to me today, like she always waves to whoever's on the register. I'm sure she doesn't know my name, but she always says hello. She reminds me a bit of my grandmother, except thinner and kookier. Also my grandma usually dressed a little nicer when she went out, even to the drug store. Mrs. Wilcox usually wears her sweats and dirty sneakers when I see her. The shoes had once been white but were darkened with dirt and starting to fall apart. She must not own a car.

She made a beeline for the alcohol aisle today, which is unusual. Most of the time she moseys around the store and maybe picks up a few things here and there. I guess today she means business. I watch her turn and disappear down the aisle and make a mental note to remember she's there. I know she'll be calling me over to help her in a few minutes.

My last customer in line leaves. I place my hands on the

register and stare down at the floor. I take a minute to stare at the dirty gray tiles, only hearing the shitty music that plays over the loudspeakers. I focus on the tips of my own dirty sneakers. My eyes start to water a little because I'm not blinking. My mind goes clear. What am I *doing-*

"Can you help me?"

There she is. Mrs. Wilcox is calling me over. She always needs help finding her wine. I wipe my face and go to help her. She is already asking me for recommendations, as if this was a five-star restaurant and I was going to tell her about the obscure tasting notes of each selection. "I don't know what to get, I don't really drink much." She says this every time she comes in. I nod like I believe her. I pick up the jug of red Carlo Rossi that she usually likes. I tell her it's a good one and it's what she got last time. She never acknowledges that there was a last time. She mumbles her thanks and then I take it to the front to ring her up.

Mrs. Wilcox talks like a simpleton, so I guess that makes her one. She always states the obvious and repeats herself a lot. She stares at you while she talks, and her large glasses and messy hair make her look crazed. I learned early on not to try to keep a conversation with her. That rule applies to a lot of people that come in the store. It's a town full of simpletons.

She's blathering to me while she pays but I'm not really taking it in. I keep nodding while she slides her debit card through the scanner. I bag her wine jug twice, although I know she'll carry it by the neck of the bottle. Which is actually smart on her part; there's no way the cheap plastic bags can hold that heavy a jug. Sure enough, she wraps the bags tight around the jug and carries it by the glass handles. She tells me to have a good weekend and shuffles out. I watch her leave, wondering what happens when she gets home. Does she start drinking by herself right away?

I remember once when Mrs. Wilcox came in and ran into her ex-daughter-in-law. It was an emotional reunion, for at least one of them. Mrs. Wilcox was so happy to see her. She said she missed the younger woman, who hugged her and told her they were still family, despite whatever happened. I stood quietly behind the counter wondering what happened to the son/husband. Divorce? Prison? Death? Military service? Felt rude to ask, so I stayed silent.

After Mrs. Wilcox left, her ex-daughter-in-law chatted to me as I rang up her cigs. "She's a sweet old lady, but she's a crazy bird." I nodded in the hopes of looking sympathetic. "I don't know," the daughter-in-law continued, "I should visit her more. Poor thing doesn't get many visitors."

How do you spend your evenings when you're a drunk or crazy? I wonder if Mrs. Wilcox gets sad. Maybe she's too crazy to really acknowledge how sad she is. Perhaps she drinks to forget. I wonder what her life looked like ten or twenty years ago. Maybe she was vibrant and happy once. Or maybe her story has always been sad.

Another older lady soon comes up to my register. She's like

the opposite of Mrs. Wilcox; she moves faster, she speaks flamboyantly, her hair and her clothes are put together. She places a bottle, not a jug or a box, of white wine on the counter, next to a pair of lady razors. She catches my eye and proudly declares, "I'm going to go home, I'm going to shave my legs, open this wine, and call my boyfriend!" I laughed with her. She's like Blanche from *The Golden Girls*. No sign of slowing down.

Some old things refuse to go out of style. Remember "film" that went into "cameras"? I didn't either until I started working here. An unsurprising amount of people in this town still use them and come here to get their photos developed. The Kodak people (or whoever) come in twice a week to pick up and drop off. It takes a while. I've explained this many times. At least once a week I tell someone that getting pictures developed takes time.

I always panic when Bitchface Johnson has photos sent out. She always comes in to check on them before they're in and complains when I don't have anything for her. I try to explain, but she just scoffs or says something nasty. She's my least favorite customer, the trash de la trash of the town. "Bitchface" isn't her Christian name; I refuse to remember her real name out of respect for myself.

Bitchface always looks pissed off, as her nickname implies. In these summer months she's usually wearing something sleeveless. Her arms are worn and leathery, too much sun exposure from walking around town all day. Her body is on the thin side; if she weren't so wrinkled she'd probably look healthy. But smoking, sunlight, and whatever other stresses that happen took their toll on her. Now she is a loud, cranky, ugly, bitchy woman who strolls around town giving horrible attitude to people. She is the epitome of what this town can do to a person.

Her tattoos stick out most of all. I don't notice most people's tats. It's second nature at this point. I see ink on arms, necks, occasionally a face. Nothing really jumps out; a few stars here, some barbed wire there. Unremarkable things. But Bitchface has something unique. Her shirts are usually low-cut and show off her dry brown cleavage. In these instances, you can see that she has a pair of eyes tattooed on her tits. That's one eye per tit.

It's not an *ugly* pair of eyes per se, but the location and person they're on make it trashy. They're somewhat blueish and yellow, like the eyes on the cover of *The Great Gatsby*. That's probably a coincidence. Her second pair of eyes match her first pair of eyes: they look angry. Bitchface is always glaring at somebody. I wonder if her tit eyes have the power to turn a man to stone.

What does one have to go through to get a pair of eyes tattooed on their boobs? I'd imagine one has to do a lot of smack to make this decision, but I shouldn't assume the worst. Although the worst is often accurate. I bet the eyes represented someone in Bitchface's life. Probably her mother. They always remember the mother, even when the mother is the cause of their problems. Her mom probably died and she got her eyes tattooed on her in her memory. Mother is always watching. Through your chest. I wonder if Bitchface ever has sex with anyone, and if they're put off (or turned on) by the tit eyes glaring at them. I bet when she's naked the eyes look sad.

A young woman often comes in with Bitchface. I assume it's her daughter. Her daughter looks tired and miserable all the time. She never speaks to me. She's pale in contrast to the burnt color of her mom. She almost always wears battered sweatshirts, even in the summertime. She looks like a character that a young Helena Bonham Carter would've won awards for playing. I pity her. She has no chance whatsoever in the world. She's just following her mom.

Sometimes when I'm bored, I'll go through peoples' photos. Yeah, I do that. Of course I do. It's so easy to get away with, just put 'em into a new envelope when you're done. No one notices. I'm curious what kind of shit people are still *mailing away* to get developed. Mostly it's boring tacky stuff. Holidays together, cookouts, camping trips. I yearn for scandalous sex pictures, just for a good laugh and a mental scarring.

Bitchface is one customer whose pictures I'll never look at it. I just think that somehow…she'll know.

Tonight I find myself awake in the middle of the night. I go out to the front porch to smoke. The street is quiet and still, no surprise there. The street is barely busy during the day.

I glance up the street at my neighbors' homes, all of them more-or-less the same. Everyone has crap in their yard, old toys and cheap decorations. The vehicles on the street are either rusty old cars or ridiculously large trucks. People here will shell out thousands of dollars they don't have for a gigantic pickup truck and then bitch a week later about gas prices.

The one neighbor down the street kept his flags on his truck tonight. One American flag, one Trump flag. He's a character. By which I mean, a huge piece of shit. Flies those tacky flags because how else would he get any kind of validation in his life? Overweight, divorced, a nice-enough paying job that he fell into. So happy and fulfilled yet spends all his free time sharing memes on Facebook.

I laugh at everyone that flies a presidential flag in this town. The idea that any political leaders have our backs is so comical. I don't think there's been a sitting U.S. President that would have used this town for anything other than wiping his nose in it. Votes are the only thing left politicians can get from the people here. They've already taken our coal, they've thrown our bodies into their wars. Votes are all we have left to give.

Sometimes I think about leaving here. Getting out of this town and never looking back. Are people in other towns and cities as downtrodden as the folks here? As a cashier I have a front row seat to how angry they are. Some of them look like they haven't smiled in years. It's hard, though, the idea of leaving. I love my mom, love my family. Love my friends, even though I hardly get to see them. Hard to say if a change of scenery would improve things.

I take a nice long drag of cigarette. I hate thinking about this shit, and it always happens when I wake up in the middle of the night. Tonight, I'm awake because of a nightmare. I don't dream often, but when I do they stick in my head for days. This one was particularly vivid.

In my dream I was late for work. I couldn't find the store even though I drive the same route every day. I kept saying, "I can't be late again, they'll fire me, this was my last strike." Already I should've known it was a dream; I'm never late in real life.

I finally found the store. After I walked through the double glass doors I saw a place entirely different from the store I'm used to. It was like a Super Walmart instead of a rinky-dink drug store. The ceilings were high as a cathedral and the shelves went all the way to the top. I couldn't see any of the walls, it was just an endless sea of shelves. The cash registers weren't up front where they should've been, so I started running through the aisles looking for them.

In the first aisle I saw Mrs. Wilcox, looking lost and confused like usual. She saw me and called out, "Can you help me? I don't know what I'm looking for." Both sides of the aisle were stocked with nothing but her favorite flavor of Carlo Rossi red wine. She had two more full jugs of the same wine in her buggy already. She looked at me with her sad bleary eyes, pleading with me to help her.

I told her I had to punch in, but I'd be right back to give her a hand. In the next aisle I saw my coworkers stocking the shelves. Becky was putting Halloween candy on one side and Pam was putting Christmas decorations on the other. They both looked at me as I approached. They were pale and had a lot of wrinkles. Like they'd been stocking those shelves for years without a break.

"They just put this stuff out earlier and earlier every year." Becky said to me, gesturing to the candy. Her voice was slow and monotone, like she was recovering from a lobotomy or something. Pam cocked her head slowly at me and spoke in a similar voice. "Shouldn't you have punched in by now?"

I nodded at them and kept running. They had scared me; I didn't know what was going on. I still couldn't see past the aisles. It felt like the store was getting darker. I just started running, I don't know if I was looking for the registers or the exit.

The next aisle was very different. Carl the FedEx guy was laying on a bed raised up on a platform, like some Egyptian pharaoh. The lights weren't the usual fluorescents. A spotlight was focused onto the bed and the rest of the aisle was in darkness. I felt like I'd interrupted a scene in a play. I panicked a bit because I didn't know my lines. Luckily there was no audience.

Carl had his sunglasses on and his boots with the white socks that went up to his knees. Besides that he was naked. He was slowly stroking a large erection and glaring at me from behind his shades-covered eyes. His other hand casually reached up to pinch a pierced nipple. His eyebrows suggestively shot up from behind his sunglasses.

"Hey," he said in a sultry porno voice. He nodded with his chin the way he usually did at the store. "I've got a package for you here."

I hesitated for a minute, taking it all in. This was a bit aggressive right? To fuck right here in the store, one of the least sexy places I can imagine trying to get off in. I opened my mouth to speak but couldn't find any words to say. The greatest hits of the early 2000s continued to play over the radio in my silence.

Carl licked his lips and spoke again. "Can you sign for this? The pen is by my leg."

I looked by his leg to, sure enough, see a black stylus next to his thigh. But his FedEx tablet was nowhere in sight. Where was I supposed to sign? This was making less and less sense. I held up a finger as if to say, "One moment, please." I backed away from him slowly, never taking my eyes off of his hand rhythmically sliding up and down his dick.

As I turned around to run away I heard him yell after me, "Hey, have a good one!"

I was now trapped in a never-ending aisle. I was running at full speed, taking in the shelves as I ran. None of it made sense: shampoo was next to bread, jugs of milk were arranged on non-refrigerated shelves. A big white sign hung off one shelf that just read "CRAP." Sales tags were all over the floor. They kept flying up at me like leaves in a windstorm.

I felt like I was getting closer to something, whatever it was I was looking for. Then I saw her: Bitchface Johnson was coming down the aisle at me. She was wearing a low-cut shirt and her shitty stained sweatpants. She looked pissed. The eyes on her breasts looked even more pissed. In her left hand I saw she was clutching a switchblade.

"Where are *you* going?" she yelled out. Her voice sounded like her usual twangy sneer mixed with the low growl of a demon.

I turned tail and ran. I knew I could never take down this bitch. She kept yelling things as I ran. I could feel that she was chasing me. What had I done wrong this time?

"You need to help me!" her voice screeched after me down the aisle.

I ran harder. Shelves full of items and sales tags whizzed by. My heart was pounding in my head.

"Help me! Help me! Help me!"

Her shrieks were getting closer; she was gaining on me. The aisle kept going and going. My legs were feeling heavy. I couldn't see the walls of the building anymore. Where was I going? What was I doing? I stopped running. There was a brief moment of peace where I couldn't hear Bitchface yelling anymore. Had I escaped?

Then I felt her jump on me and take me down to the ground. I twisted my body as I fell so I landed on my back. All I could see in front of my face were her breast-eyes. They were glaring at me, a living beast. I heard a growl somewhere right before the switchblade came down into my stomach.

Of course, that was the moment I jerked awake. I realized I was breathing hard and I was sweating. My hands automatically reached down to my gut to check for a stab wound, which was stupid of course. Satisfied that there was no knife in me, I cursed Bitchface for haunting my dreams and got out of bed.

Now I flick my cigarette butt off the porch into the yard. I make a mental note to pick all the butts out of there before Mom starts bitching about it. I stand here for a few minutes, just glaring out at the empty street. I don't want to go back to bed; I don't want to feel trapped again.

I hate working Sunday mornings. For a day meant to be holy, people sure are a pain in the ass. Sundays are the days you're more likely to hear "Can I talk to the manager?" or a general cuss word directed at you. I hate Sundays. I think we should just close like all the restaurants in town. But what do I know?

The most annoying part of Sunday comes at one o'clock. You can't sell alcohol until after one on a Sunday in the state of West Virginia. So at 12:55 every Sunday you can usually find a line of people just waiting to buy booze. Some of them come every week. We stare at each other until one. They know how it works. Some customers who aren't in the know will complain. I calmly explain to them how the computer won't let me ring up their alcohol until one. Even if I wanted to, I couldn't make their sale. They sneer and tell me that's stupid, as if I governed the law.

As much as I hate this law, I hate these people more. There are just a few hours of the entire week when you can't buy alcohol here: nine to one on a Sunday. Four hours out of my whole week. You chose to try to buy alcohol at the wrong time and now you're mad at me? Sure, it's a stupid rule, but it's a rule you know about. There's no reason to give me attitude about it. There's no reason at all.

My Sunday shift is shorter today. A four-hour shift is barely worth getting out of bed for. At least it's over quickly. But Sunday always brings a new week. I look at my schedule for the coming week but don't register it: it's just numbers on a sheet, same as always. I take a picture of it with my phone to look at later.

At about one-thirty our next-door neighbors come in. Not the neighbors at my house; the store's neighbors. They live in a trailer on a small dirt lot behind the store. I don't know how things like that happen, why their trailer isn't with the others in the trailer park at the south end of town. I also don't know how long they've been here. It's none of my business, and despite my curiosity I actually don't care. They're very familiar with my coworkers, but I've never bothered to learn their names.

Their close proximity means they're constantly coming into the store to pick up a roll of toilet paper or a bag of chips. Their skin is perpetually dirty like they just finished working on a construction site. Their usual year-round outfit is a heavy jacket thrown over a t-shirt paired with sweatpants. In their defense, that's a pretty common look around town. Their clothes are dirty too, but somehow they never have a stench on them. It's like dirt is just who they are, it's ingrained into their appearance. It may be impossible for them to get squeaky-clean at this point.

The woman has a very masculine face and keeps her hair cut short. She never wears makeup and if I hadn't met her when she was eight months pregnant I would've mistaken her for a man. After her pregnancy she went back to smoking a pipe. For my sake I pretend she always smokes outside the trailer while her baby is inside. I remember the day she brought the new baby into the store to show Becky and Pam. It was a surprisingly cute baby wrapped in a blanket from the hospital, probably the cleanest garment in their house at the time.

As far as trailer trash go, they're better than most. Very friendly people, never caused a problem in the store. They always look exhausted, even before their baby was born. Eyelids sitting heavy over glossy eyes, underlined by the dark bags. It's the look of someone who's in a constant struggle with life. I see it on a lot of people every day. Perpetually tired-looking and dirty. But they're alright. The only time I want to avoid them is when they're buying a lice kit, which unfortunately happens fairly often.

The neighbors wave to me as they walk in, and I return it

politely. As soon as they disappear down the aisle another couple walks in. They're younger, and they're also trash. The girl is one of those girls that just looks so repressed. Like her soul was removed and now she's just a body with bad posture and gray sweatshirts. Her boyfriend has a dumb-looking face and wears a stained wife-beater. She heads back to the pharmacy while her boyfriend approaches me at the front counter. He is holding a leaking plastic cup from a gas station. Guessing from the distinct lime-green color, I think it had once been a Mountain Dew slushie.

"Hey," he says to me, "you got a nackin' back there? This thing's drippin'!" I notice he is missing his front teeth. Good thing he's taking care of his remaining teeth by drinking Mountain Dew.

I told him I didn't have any nackins but here is a paper towel. He took it without thanking me, wiped the shit off the sides of the cup, and handed the dirty wet towel back to me to throw away. He then left to join his girlfriend by the pharmacy. I wonder why he didn't wait outside with his leaky cup. I take more paper towels and lay them on the ground to soak up what he'd dripped on the floor. I push them around with my foot, cursing this stupid fangless animal.

It's unfair to see ugly people dating. I wonder if it feels good to her when he kisses her with that mouth. Can she fit her tongue in the gap between his teeth? A mouth like that has got to taste of pop and Doritos twenty-four/seven. I bet he feels lucky to have her, how he relishes every little second he can get her to crack a small smile. Maybe he's the only person who can make her laugh. I wonder if they're happy together. I worry that they're happier than I am.

The weeks go by, and not much changes around here. I am working the afternoon shift today so I decide to spend the morning applying for jobs. I fill out a few online applications, entering and reentering all my job experience and exaggerated skills. Then, per Mom's suggestion, I drop my resume off at a few places. It's an old-fashioned suggestion, but some of these places are still so old-fashioned they accept paper resumes.

Most of the places I apply to don't really seem like better alternatives to the drug store, but you can never be too sure. There's got to be a job out there behind a desk or in a warehouse that I'm qualified for. I don't wanna become a lifer at the drug store. I can't shake the feeling that I won't want to become a lifer at any of these places either.

Finding a job to do for life sounds like finding a spouse. How are you ever sure that it's forever? I guess when you know, you just know. Yet people get divorced and laid off all the time. Nothing is ever really certain. I feel a pull of dread washing over me as I drive to work, so I light a cigarette to make myself feel better. I feel better for as long as the cigarette lasts.

I park at work. I am a little early so I go inside for a Diet Coke. I wave to Pam as I walk in. She gives me a sarcastic smile. Pam is kind of a curmudgeon. Does she get a sense of dread before coming to work too? Or is she just used to it by now?

I bring my bottle of pop up to the front and have Pam ring me up. "Did you hear, honey?" she asks as she applies the employee discount. I shake my head. "Mrs. Wilcox died last night."

Oh. Grief for a practical stranger is a weird thing. I felt bad for Mrs. Wilcox, but then I had always felt bad for Mrs. Wilcox. Her life had never seemed appealing to me. I thought she was horribly unhappy. But now she was gone, and she wouldn't have to be unhappy anymore.

I sit in my car, drinking my pop and smoking. I wonder how many people would go to her funeral, where she would be buried. Her ex-daughter-in-law would probably show up. Maybe her son would get to attend the services, get an escort out of prison or something. If that's where he is; I never did find out. For all I know he is dead too. I guess I could find out in the obituary.

Pam didn't know how she'd passed away, but it could be any number of health issues. Or maybe just a freak accident. I thought of all the glass jugs of Carlo Rossi I'd sold her and had to shake off the feeling that I may have somehow unwittingly played a hand in her death. I mean, I know I'm not technically responsible, she's an adult who is allowed to buy alcohol. I wonder if drug dealers who sell someone their last fix ever feel guilty about it.

Shortly after I clock in, in walks Bitchface Johnson. I feel my neck tighten as I remember my dream, still hearing her terrible yelling. I brace myself for whatever could possibly happen: does she have pictures out, are her pictures not in, is she going to stab me to death, am I going to die in this store like Patty? Her face is unreadable as ever, but at least today she's wearing a hoodie so the tit eyes are covered. But I know they're there.

But it's simple today. A bag of Skittles and a Mountain Dew. Sugar fix. She pays with a five. I ask if she needs a bag. "Nah." I give her the change and toss the receipt when she waves it away.

"Have a nice day" I say. I wonder if I sound sincere, because this is one of those rare moments where I really do mean it.

"Thanks, you too." She says it all without smiling, without changing the tone in her voice. But for her, this is as close to pleasant as we can get. I'm just happy not to be stabbed.

Later Carl the FedEx guy comes in. It's payday and he's dropping off the checks. I sign for the delivery, and he starts his usual small talk. It is such a nice day today, blah blah blah. I nod as I scribble out my signature. As he takes back his little tablet thing I feel him staring at me. I blush a bit as I remember my erotic nightmare; the spotlight, the music, the nipple piercings.

"Are you okay?"

I try to look into his eyes behind those thick sunglasses. I imagine his eyes are full of concern, that he is somehow seeing into my soul.

"I'm not sure." I shrug.

"Oh," Carl says. "Well I hope you feel better soon."

"Thanks."

He nods, says a quiet "Yup" and goes to leave. I watch him reach the first set of glass automatic doors. I raise my voice to reach him before he exits. "Have a good day!"

He turns back to me, smiles his toothy grin, and shoots me with his finger gun. "Have a good one."

ACKNOWLEDGEMENTS

I'll thank my family first on this page, as their support for every silly thing I do has gotten me this far and they should get the credit for that. I'll thank my friends second, both the ones I have now and the ones I've lost touch with. These stories could not have been written without any of you.

Thanks to Moundsville, West Virginia. I grew up there, so you're responsible for these stories too, like it or not.

Self-publishing means I don't have a list of agents and editors to rave about. But a special thank you goes to Jodi, Tara, and Jessica for being my beta readers, letting me bounce ideas off them, and passing along information about self-publishing (I'm still learning!). Thank you to Jonathon for making the cover and putting up with my questions.

Thank you to you for reading this collection, I really hope you liked it.